Pan and the
Message Chair

Pan and the Message Chair

Lawrence Weill

Seventh Star
Press

Cover design: Olivia Pro Design

Cover art in this book copyright © 2023 Olivia Pro Design and Seventh Star Press, LLC.

Editor: Stephen Zimmer

Published by Seventh Star Press, LLC.

ISBN Number: 979-8-3964910-9-0

Seventh Star Press

www.seventhstarpress.com

info@seventhstarpress.com

Publisher's Note:

Pan and the Message Chair is a work of fiction. All names, characters, and places are the product of the author's imagination, used in fictitious manner. Any resemblances to actual persons, places, locales, events, etc. are purely coincidental.

Printed in the United States of America

First Edition

In memory of Jennie

Chapter 1

Rain pattered on hickory, oak, and poplar leaves, matted into a monochromatic carpet from deep, dark brown to pale ochre. Where the winter wind had swept clearings in the forest, bright green clumps of moss carried red spore crowns that crept the moss inexorably up rotting corpses of trees felled by the axes of wind, ice, and time.

The grey-black trunks of their progeny jutted into the grey-white sky, reaching for a sun that seemingly refused to shine, until spring willed itself into the woods. In a few weeks, those branches would press tiny buds of a new year's canopy onto their fingertips, but now, only cold rain traced along those veinless hands. The rain wicked its way from twig to branch to limb to trunk and, finally, to root, where the slumbering giants drank it up, awaiting only their cue from the earth to push it back up into leaves. A cold song of wind whispered through the timbers. Up the hill, a pileated woodpecker hammered out a rhythm, *rat-a-tat-a-tat-a-tat-a*, then sent out its jungle bird aria and flew to a nearby black gum to pick up the rhythm again.

Old Raliv leaned back under the shed roof as a gust of cold air brought a bracing splash of rain onto his face. The drops barely made a sound on the mossy shingles of the shelter where he stood.

He traced a figure up the hillside with his gaze. He knew every knob of each stump, where the angles from a fallen shag

1

bark, stripped clean by ladderbacks and deer, left a tunnel in the undergrowth. Something new was there, a small round bump above a chunk of sandstone dislodged from the root-ball of a felled giant.

Then it was gone, ducked down in an instant.

Raliv's subtle movement had startled it, but it hadn't fled. A turkey, no doubt, scraping the woods for fallen mast from the autumn before. Raliv considered raising his rifle while it wasn't watching, but then it was back, just as suddenly as it had disappeared before.

Then there was a different turkey, scratching its way through the woods. Then another. It was a hen and juvenile group. There would be no toms in this group yet, and while the younger ones were no longer poults, Raliv would not try to take any of these.

They were just starting out. He couldn't see taking their lives for the few stringy morsels they would bring. He still didn't move, didn't want to frighten them off, even if he was not going to shoot at them.

He watched as they moved from behind the pile of rocks and roots, making their way towards the beaver pond below, scratching, stepping. There were eight, Raliv counted. In a month, or maybe even less, the toms would be with them and maybe he could take one, but not now.

Raliv watched them make their way down the hillside and disappear into the fowl manna grass and bulrushes that bordered the flats, then returned his gaze into the woods. A phoebe landed on a twig hanging near him, cocked his head this way, that way, as if studying him, then flitted off in the direction of the feeder he had filled that morning with cracked dried corn and a bent-over, dried sunflower head.

On a red oak twenty yards away, a grey squirrel climbed headfirst down the trunk. That would do for dinner. Raliv raised his gun and fired in a split second, the squirrel plopping lifeless onto the forest floor. The sharp report of the gun still echoed through the woods.

Now the woods were quiet, the woodland song stifled for

the moment by the pop of the .22. But even before Raliv could step forward to retrieve the squirrel, a nuthatch gave out its grunting call on the shelf of an oak bough. A breeze returned the susurrous sighings to the forest.

Raliv cleaned the squirrel, saving the tail to trade for fishing lures, and left the four segments of meat in a bowl of cold salty water. He walked over to the woodstove, opened the firebox, and tossed in three split pieces of maple from the small woodpile next to the door.

Leaning over, he blew on the coals below the sticks and a small flame popped up. He grabbed a heavy iron skillet from the warming shelf and placed it on the stove top and reached over to feel the water heater. He touched it gingerly at first, just in case it was hot, but quickly realized it would not be that hot with the fire reduced to embers from his breakfast of rolled oats. Still, it was warm, which pleased him. He placed a metal basin below the spigot and let out just enough warm water to clean up in. Raliv cooked the squirrel in a pouring of bacon grease he had saved in an emptied soup can.

Outside, the rain had stopped, but the sky was still grey, heavy with water waiting to fall. The light from the oil lamp was meager, but enough to fry up a squirrel in. He plated the meat and a scoop of beans from the night before onto a chipped plate, added several thick slices of red onion, and sat in a stiff, ladder-back chair at the end of the drop leaf table.

Before he ate, he looked up at the other end of the little table, where Colleen, his wife, would have been sitting. But she wasn't there, of course. No matter how intensely Raliv willed his wife to be with him, death would not ever release her or him.

Under the table, Felicity rubbed against his foot and gave out a single meow, her way of reminding him to share his meal. Colleen had taken in the calico when it showed up at their farmhouse near the highway, and although Raliv had been lukewarm on the idea of taking in a pet, he was glad now for the company. It made little sense, of course, to be painfully lonely and yet to retreat to this old hunting cabin they had built on the back end of their spread.

If he had stayed at the farmhouse, he could get into town more easily, could have visitors, maybe family, coming to check up on him, or even religious folks, arriving to convince him to join their church. He had no intentions of going to their church, or any church, for that matter. What would be the point of praying to a God that would allow him to be so miserable, so angry, so alone? But he could have at least talked to the missionaries, had human conversation, even if it was to tell them that it was their God who had left him, not the other way around.

Raliv pulled apart some of the meat and leaned down to put some in the cat's dinner bowl. She watched him, almost nonchalantly, but hurried over when he straightened back up in his chair. He looked down at his plate, a specimen from a set Colleen had culled. It was a simple earthenware dish from a potter in eastern Kentucky, glazed with blue and white. Colleen had collected dishes, always finding a new favorite pattern that was her everyday china, until another set caught her eye. She had given away at least a half-dozen full sets to their sons and to nephews and nieces over the years, and placed boxes of dishes inside the charity box in town.

He ate his dinner slowly, deliberately. There was no hurry. There was nothing to do, no place to be. Raliv decided he would bring a radio out next time he went to town, something to break the overwhelming silence. Then, he wondered if they even made battery powered radios anymore. He cleaned up after dinner, washing both his own plate and Felicity's bowl. Pouring himself a draught of bourbon in a juice glass, he set it on a small table across the room next to the fireplace.

After throwing on a couple of logs, he poked around with a metal rod until the fire blazed up, then sat in an overstuffed chair and sipped the bitter liquor, watching the flames dance along the logs. Felicity jumped into his lap, made an awkward circle around his legs, then lay down, purring. He looked at the mismatched chair next to him, where Colleen should be sitting, humming a tune she had heard on the radio that day, or reading by the light of a kerosene lamp.

Nighttime was the hardest.

During the day, there were tasks to be completed, various menial chores that he had procrastinated on before, but now he took them on, welcoming the chance to complete something, to repair even little items that were broken. Fixing the latch on the pantry door meant he didn't stop to think about his wife, his best friend, his partner, being gone, whisked away in just a few months, before he could even truly comprehend what was happening to her.

Even at the end, they had dared to make plans, dream about what they would be doing in spring, what seeds to pick up at the farm store in town to plant, even travel plans. It was time to start the broccoli and cauliflower seeds indoors, but somehow, Raliv just didn't see the point. What difference did it make? It wouldn't be long before the chickweed and lambsquarters came up. He knew where morels came up each year, and they should be up very soon.

There was plenty of game, and the pond was actually underfished, so he could survive out here, alone, for a long time. Not that he needed to live like that. He had a decent pension coming in, but maybe it would be easier just to hide, to run away from all of it. He wasn't sure if anyone would even notice he was not around. Who would notice if Raliv just moved permanently to the cabin and just disappeared?

He turned to Colleen's chair, the question almost on his lips, and then caught himself up short. His eyes filled with tears that overflowed and ran down his cheeks. He pictured Colleen sitting there, her hair, still dark although she never colored it, curling around her face, framing her soft features.

He glanced up at the rough-hewn mantle and the photo he had brought from the house, a simple shot of the two of them on a trip just last spring down to Bonita Springs with friends. He and Colleen had found themselves on their own one day and had driven down to Lover's Key, where they had taken the little trolley over to the beach and had just sat there on the sand, no beach gear at all, and enjoyed each other's company and the sun and the water. They had watched children splashing in the small waves and seen porpoises swimming by, lazily.

He had taken a selfie of the two of them, her leaning against his back, close, holding him by the shoulder and smiling self-contentedly. Going back to the car, they had watched manatees swim in the little estuary and then had spent the rest of the afternoon eating shrimp and drinking wine at a bayside restaurant overlooking a small marina. It was how they always enjoyed travel, at their own pace, doing whatever seemed natural to do.

"I love you," he whispered to the picture.

"I miss you," he said to the chair now.

A log shifted in the fireplace and sent a spray of sparks up the chimney, catching his attention. Raliv returned his stare to the fire. He took another sip of bourbon and felt his sorrow turn to anger yet again. He often found himself on this precipice, somewhere between heavy sadness and fiery anger. Watching the fire for a long time, he waited for it to wither, and when he had finished his drink, the fire had burned down to embers.

He lifted Felicity off his lap and, as if his lifting reminded her she suddenly wanted something desperately in the other room, she flipped herself upright and bolted from his hands. Crossing the room to the bed, he pulled off his clothes and put on his heavy flannel pajamas, although he kept his socks on, knowing the room would be chilly by morning, and even the oblong rag rug by the bed would be a cold shock to his feet.

He looked at his reflection in the small, wood-framed mirror beside the bed. The face that looked back looked tired, gaunt. He had lost some thirty pounds during Colleen's illness, being too distracted and too worried to eat much, and his grey beard had grown out to the point of scraggle, to match his unkempt hair.

Shaking his head at the image, he then crawled under the covers on one side of the bed, his side, and looked at the empty pillows next to him. He reached over and extinguished the oil lamp and lay in bed, trying to sleep. He didn't know how long he lay there, but finally he slept. It was the same every night. Once he fell asleep, he slept until morning, but falling asleep was hard.

Raliv awoke the next morning to a stream of sunlight blasting through the small window above the bed. He sat up and looked out the window. A slight breeze shook the few stubborn remaining leaves from last year on the sugar maple, but it looked warm. It might not be, of course, but Raliv was eager to get out in the sunlight. It seemed like a very long time since he had seen the brightness.

He crawled out of bed and stoked the fire in the cookstove, then dressed as the coffee pot began its gurgling percolating. As soon as he was dressed, he opened the door and stepped through the screen door. It was warm. Not full-fledged spring day warm, maybe, but much better than the cold rain that had fallen for weeks, it seemed.

Over on the next ridge, a train whistle blew, and Raliv could hear the rhythm of the coal cars, clunk-clunking across the crossing. He retreated to the cabin, poured a cup of inky coffee, and grabbed a tin of kippered herring from the pantry.

He went back outside and sat at the picnic table in the clearing that Colleen had turned into a little woodland garden. She liked bulbs and corms, planting a few more each year to supplement the natural spreading of plants, as well as adding variety. She was happiest when nesting. Raliv gave an appreciative glance at the profusion of green shoots coming up.

Sitting backwards at the table, using the rough tabletop as a backrest, he surveyed the woods and shoveled salty fish into his mouth. He washed it down with the earthy, bitter coffee. Colleen's crocuses pushed delicate yellow and purple blooms up through the brown leaves. Daffodils were also sending up full heads, ready to add to the yellow. Irises jutted stiff leaves up but wouldn't send their bloom stalks up until later.

Felicity meowed from behind the screen door. Raliv saved a bit of fish for the cat. "You hungry?" Raliv croaked out. He hadn't spoken in his full voice in so long, it was as if his throat was uncertain how to carry it off. Felicity stretched her front legs out then plopped over on her side for Raliv to pet her. He opened the screen and pet Felicity, then placed the remaining fish in the cat's bowl, tapping the last bits into the metal dish. He rinsed out the can, put it in the recycling bag, and put on a jacket.

Raliv picked up his .22 and headed back out, closing Felicity in and the world out with the heavy wooden door. He wasn't planning on hunting especially, but he wanted to be ready if something presented itself. Crossing the little yard, he headed into the forest.

The sun turned everything brighter. Shadows stretched across the leaves. A large bird flew between him and the sun, throwing a shadow across him. Perhaps a buzzard heading for the entrails of the squirrel he had left at the bottom of the hill. Raliv walked around the hillside and climbed up towards where the old power line had been. The line was long dead, but the wide path the electric company had cleared would make for easier walking.

He could see the open area at the top of the hill and quickened his pace, eager to be in full sunlight. Up ahead, a white throated sparrow sang out, "Old Sam Peabody Peabody Peabody." Probably in one of the scruffy junipers that had volunteered in the clearing.

Raliv glanced ahead, as if to see the bird, but knew he was farther away than that. In speeding up, he became less cautious and suddenly stepped into a hole hidden by the fallen leaves, sending him to his hands and knees and tossing the rifle to the ground in front of him. He stood back up slowly.

He wasn't hurt, thankfully, but he knew better, and he recriminated himself for being in a hurry. Gathering himself, he leaned over to retrieve his gun, but then saw something that he had not seen before.

A branch was pulled down at an angle it should not be and attached to it was a cord. He followed the cord with his eyes. It looked like several shoelaces tied together, and at the end was a loop tied to a stick. Some rocks had been piled around to encourage the would-be prey into the snare.

Someone was on his land, setting a trap for a rabbit. Maybe there were more snares. Raliv looked around for more bent-over branches. No, this was the only one. He walked closer and looked at the trap. It looked like it would work. He was tempted to spring the trap, since someone should really ask before coming onto his land and setting a trap, but he stopped himself. He wanted to see this person and confront them for trespassing, for taking his game, and then shoo them off, so he walked around the trap and made the last few feet into the open field.

The sun poured down like warm water, and he stood still for a moment, basking, his face upturned into the light. The sunlight stroked his face like a warm blanket. There was a breeze that whispered through the oaks and sycamores of the woods behind him. The sunlight was so welcome, he almost forgot his intent, almost forgot his peevishness at someone being on his place without permission.

He and Colleen had joked about being the sort of older couple who might sit in their rockers on the porch of their farmhouse, shotguns at the ready, yelling, "Get off my lawn" to anyone who ventured down the long drive to their home. The truth was, Colleen was more of the one to embrace just being with Raliv and no one else, unless it was the grandchildren, of course. Colleen had embraced being Nana with ardor she didn't always let others see.

Raliv shook himself out of his reverie and stepped over to a stand of lespedeza that should provide a hiding spot for him. Before squatting down to wait for the culprit to make himself known, Raliv glanced back over to be sure he could see the trap, but he couldn't find it. He looked for the bent branch where he thought it should be, but there instead was a rabbit, hanging from the snare, kicking.

Even better, thought Raliv. Now he would not only catch this thief red-handed, he would have hasenpfeffer for dinner. He tried to stay in a squatting position, but his legs quickly grew tired of that, so he leaned back somewhat awkwardly and sat on the soft ground.

Repositioning his .22 in his lap, he looked over at the ensnared rabbit, or at where it had been a few moments ago, but it was gone. The shoelaces were gone too. The branch was bobbing, just a bit. He had missed them, whoever they were.

He struggled to get his feet beneath himself, then trotted over to the tree. Then it occurred to him that whoever had set the trap was watching it, knew it had been sprung, and thus knew to retrieve the rabbit. That also meant they had seen Raliv.

Looking through the woods for signs of movement, there was only a soft swaying of tree limbs, a flutter from a leaf, barely holding onto its milkweed vine. He felt a shiver go up his spine. Crows called to each other, somewhere back in the woods.

It was true Raliv wasn't as spry as he had once been, but there was little that went on in the woods that he didn't know about, yet he had been out-sleuthed by this poacher, and they had been watching him. There was only one passable road on their property. Raliv walked quickly back towards the cabin.

He would retrieve his truck and drive back towards the farmhouse and find out who it was that way. He wanted to run back to his pickup, but knew running with all the traps of holes and stumps hidden beneath the leaves was far too risky. If he fell again like he had before. next to the snare, he might hurt himself, and who knew how long he might be outside, injured. Who would miss him?

He kept his focus on the forest floor as he made his way. Accustomed to moving stealthily, quietly, barely making a sound in the woods, he now stomped through the woods, crunching leaves, hearing the swishing of his canvas pants against brambles and the snap of twigs beneath his feet. It sounded like a herd of water buffalo tromping through the woods. When he made the clearing in front of the cabin, he picked up his pace and trotted over to the truck, but once he sat in the cab, he had to take a second and catch his breath.

Then he started up the rusty truck with its camper top that no longer kept water out. Turning around, he headed up the road that led through the valley and back up the hill to their farmhouse and, beyond that, the long drive that led to the highway that went to town, where Raliv had avoided for several weeks.

He wasn't sure why he stayed out on his own. He didn't dislike the people. Somehow, he didn't feel like he ought to be burdening them with his grief. People in town were pleasant to him, and just after Colleen had died, he had had to go into town to take care of arrangements and the estate, such as it was.

Since they owned everything together, it was pretty straightforward. And the people in town had looked at Raliv with tender eyes, their heads cocked slightly to one side in sympathy. They had expressed their condolences and assured Raliv that if there was anything they could do, and so forth. But there was nothing to do but to try to live, try to adjust, try to find his way in this very unfamiliar terrain.

Raliv drove along the road, more path than road, really. It was still muddy from all the rain, so he often found himself spinning a little sideways in some big puddle, but he saw no other tire tracks. It would be impossible for someone to have driven back onto his property and leave no tire tracks. At one dry spot, Raliv stopped the truck and got out, walked over to the next wide puddle, and inspected it, but there was nothing: no tire tracks, no footprints, nothing.

He looked around him, as if he might catch the culprit, still spying on him, but there was nothing and the rumbling of the truck had quieted the natural sounds of the woods. He got back in the truck and sped towards the puddle, letting momentum help push him through the boggiest spots. Once through the puddle, the road became better defined through the Johnson grass of the meadow and through the opening in the fence that had once held cattle in. He might as well check on the house, as long as he was out.

Raliv pulled onto the gravel drive before the house, the crunching of the rocks giving a warm, familiar sound. Whenever anyone came by, the sound of the gravel being shifted was an early warning system both he and Colleen had learned to listen for.

They didn't get that many visitors. Their sons and grandchildren, sometimes, but they always called first.

Occasionally the mailman drove all the way back to their house with a box to deliver, dishes ordered online. Colleen's sister was about the only other person who showed up unannounced, except for the missionaries that used to come by, but the last time they had come, Raliv had told them he was a druid, and they had not come back. Raliv really wasn't a druid, he didn't suppose, although he did appreciate the notion of harmony with the world around him, but the poor missionary, a well-scrubbed skinny girl wearing a flowered dress too large for her had not known what to say and had simply left. Raliv considered his tactic a success.

Raliv went in through the kitchen door. Inside, he took off his muddy boots by the back door and hung his jacket on the hook. The kitchen looked the same, which was good and bad. He was glad everything was in order, but looking at the kitchen table, maple with sliding leaves they pulled out when guests came, reminded him of Colleen and how many meals they had eaten there together over the years.

Raliv felt his stomach tighten. He decided he needed to do something, anything, to keep from going back into the sorrow he couldn't bear. "I need a shower," he said aloud, and his voice sounded odd, spoken in absence of anyone but himself to hear it, echoing in the room as if to remind him he was alone.

He walked through the room and down the hallway that led to their bedroom and the bathroom. As he passed the bedroom, he looked in and saw the bed, neatly made. He should sleep here tonight, he decided. He had food in the pantry and in the freezer. He should try again to sleep in their home.

Then he stopped and looked up. "Felicity," he said aloud. He turned around to go back and get the cat. He couldn't leave her locked up in the little cabin, and she was not allowed to go outside and kill the birds he fed. He retreated to the kitchen.

"Someone's been poaching rabbits on our land, Honey." He spoke to the chair where Colleen would sit for dinner as he pulled his boots back on. "Don't know how they came in, though. No tire tracks. And they are sneaky too." He stood and retrieved the jacket from the hook. "But I'll catch them, Honey. Don't you worry." He looked at the chair again before heading out. He drove up to the mailbox first and pulled out the week's worth of bills and junk mail and tossed them onto the passenger seat next to the .22 he had left there, then headed back towards the cabin.

As he crossed the meadow just before the woods, he glanced over and saw the chair they had hewn from one of the big poplars they had had to have cut by the cabin because it leaned precariously over the little house. The timber cutter had said he could shape it with his chainsaw to look like a chair, and Colleen decided it would be perfect next to the shallow pond where they had planted a holly tree and still more daffodil bulbs.

Raliv's glance at the chair had been perfunctory, but something caught his eye. There was something resting on the chair, a small animal maybe, but that wasn't right. It was too flat to be an animal. It was furry, but not full. He stopped the truck, sending the mail sliding to the floor, and backed up to get a better look.

Putting the truck in park, he got out. As he got closer to the roughly carved chair, he saw that it was a rabbit pelt. He picked it up. In fact, it was several rabbit pelts sewn together with strips of tanned rabbit leather. He held it up to inspect it. It was a bag made from rabbit skins.

He looked around him. Who put this here? And why? He looked back at the seat where he had found the rabbit bag, as if the chair would maybe give up the secret, and saw a piece of paper folded up and stuffed into a crevice that the chainsaw had left. Putting the bag down, he retrieved the note and carefully unfolded the paper. It was half an envelope, torn open carefully. On it was written in square, block letters:

I don't take more than I need. You
have lots of rabbits.

Raliv looked around himself sharply. He was certain he
was being watched, but he could see no one. He felt that chill
go up his back again. He put the note in his jacket pocket and
headed towards the truck, searching the tree line with his eyes.
Where were they? Who were they?

When he got to the truck, he looked back at the bag on the
chair. It was payment, he realized. Whoever this was, giving him
the bag was payment for the rabbit. Or rabbits, it now seemed
certain. He went back and retrieved the bag and inspected it
more closely. It was good tanning and surprisingly supple. He
liked the look of it. He went back to the truck and put the rabbit
bag in the glove box, so Felicity wouldn't freak out, and drove
back to the cabin.

Raliv loaded the cat into the small carrier. In truth, Felicity
did not try to go outside now that she had food, warmth, and
company indoors, but her dislike of being in the truck was
visceral, and he had learned to put her in the little kennel the
hard way. The scratches up and down his right arm had taken
weeks to heal.

As he was lowering Felicity into the box, the note fell
from his shirt pocket and Raliv decided on a new strategy. After
latching the wire door shut, he went over to the drop front desk
at the foot of the bed and retrieved a small notepad he had
picked up from the local weekly newspaper office. He grabbed a
pen from the drawer and wrote:

Who are you?

He started to write more, something along the lines of
stop trespassing, but he realized that it was really only a written
version of "Keep off my lawn," so decided not to write it. Then,
he added:

Pan and the Message Chair

```
Thanks for the rabbit bag. What is
your name? Where do you live?
```

Then he paused and added:

```
This is private property, you know.
```

Maybe he did want to tell them to keep off his lawn. Folding up the note, he put it in his shirt pocket. That should do it. He picked up the pet carrier and walked out the door. He rarely locked the cabin, since anyone heading this far back on their land had to pass right by the farmhouse, but this time he took out his key and set the deadbolt.

After placing the loudly meowing calico onto the passenger seat, he drove back out the path. When he got to the chair, he pulled up and turned the engine off. The day was warming nicely. Chorus frogs called from the pond. The dried-up baskets from last year's Queen Anne's lace bobbed in a slow breeze. The daffodils here in the sunlight had already started blooming.

He made his way to the chair to leave the note. He stood beside the stump. How many times had he and Colleen come here with a sandwich she had made in the kitchen and a couple of bottles of water to have an impromptu picnic, both of them managing to sit on the wide seat? They would talk about planting more flowers and maybe adding another tree. They would watch the osprey aerie atop the abandoned utility pole, a tightly woven mass of sticks, looking for the heads of the nestlings, then follow their progress to chicks, then grow to be fledglings. The same pair returned year after year, and Raliv and Colleen watched them raise their brood each year like happy grandparents.

The memory caught him up.

He sat suddenly on the seat. He looked up across the field to the nesting site atop the pole. An osprey flew to it just as he looked, carrying a stick in its talons. "Look!" Raliv pointed, then dropped his hand and let out a deep sob.

Leaning over, he buried his face into his hands and cried,

letting out deep moans and wails. Somehow, out here in the fields of wildflowers and tall grasses, it seemed a perfect place to let out some sorrow. When he had cried for several minutes, he found himself stopping, somewhere between spent and sated, for the moment.

He stood and walked towards the truck, then remembered the note in his pocket. He thought about just forgetting it. What difference would it make? Maybe he should call the sheriff and have him help catch this intruder. But then he thought about the rabbit bag, and the note left for him, and turned around and walked back over to the big stump chair. He pulled the note from his pocket, folded it up, and wedged it into the crevice where he had found his note.

Returning to the truck, he drove Felicity back to the farmhouse.

Chapter 2

T he next morning, Raliv had chores to do. For one thing, there were several bills that needed to be paid in the accumulated mail, so he would need to write out some checks, and put them in envelopes and take them to the post office. Colleen had handled most of the bill paying and usually did so online, but Raliv was new to that. Still, he vowed to figure it out.

And Felicity's gravity-fed feeder was low, so he needed to run by the farm store for cat food. At the cabin, the cat ate whatever Raliv ate, but here, she only ate dry food. She had been a stray when Colleen had taken her in, but she took to domestication easily, more easily than Raliv himself had, he would have to admit. And Colleen had tamed Raliv with tenderness and love, the same way she had coaxed the gentle calico from the frightened, hissing, straggled cat underneath the steps of the back porch that day several years ago now.

Before meeting Colleen and falling for her wit and charm, like any man would have, Raliv had not hissed but grumbled. And he had not been frightened, exactly, more like skittish. If in his early romantic endeavors he had been too vulnerable and been hurt repeatedly, he entered this relationship timidly and had found the one woman he could drop all caution before.

Raliv found himself bustling, making coffee, and grabbing a breakfast bar. The sky out the window above the sink was

17

cloudy again, yesterday's sunshine being only a brief respite, but the room was bright. Colleen's choice of the bright yellow paint ensured the room was cheery, even on the dreariest days.

He needed to go by the grocery too, perhaps. Some eggs, fresh vegetables, maybe some milk, if he thought the grandchildren might come by. His list of tasks to complete grew. Leaning against the counter, he jotted down the list on a pad of paper. He liked writing down a list and crossing each item off as he completed it. But what he realized he really wanted to do was check the chair in the pasture, to see if there was a note from the rabbit bag person. He looked out the window above the sink, in the direction of the big chair, but it was too far away for him to see from the house.

But first things first, he decided. Sitting at the kitchen table, he sorted out the bills and scrawled out the payments. On about half of them, he wrote the wrong year and had to write over his error. He shoved them into envelopes and put the stamps on them. Taking his .22 from where he had leaned it against the wall by the back door, he locked it in the narrow gun safe in their bedroom, his bedroom, he realized suddenly.

Then he grabbed his coat and picked his keys off the hook behind the door, the screw that held it in pulling out just a little, and headed out. He tossed the pile of envelopes on the seat and they slid across and onto the floor.

Then he remembered the rabbit bag was still in the glove box. Pulling it out, he placed the bills inside and put it on the passenger seat. Perfect. He was amazed at how soft the bag was. This was no amateur tanning here. Whoever this person was, he or she knew how to tan a rabbit pelt. Raliv started up the truck and headed into town.

Trips to town had become something of a rarity since Colleen had passed. He drove by the mailbox to drop the bills in, to avoid the postmaster, who had an uncanny knack of knowing everyone's name almost immediately once they started getting mail, though he used their first names as surnames, calling them "Mister Raliv" and "Miz Colleen." It was a gift, remembering everyone's name, perhaps made easier because the community was so small, but a gift, nonetheless.

Raliv liked being called by name, since this was Colleen's hometown, not his, and he always felt a little bit of the stranger, even after living here for twenty years. Still, he thought being Mr. Raliv made him sound like he ran a hair salon or something, rather than his actual job as a math teacher before he retired. But he didn't want to talk to the postmaster, or anyone else. They would just say they were sorry, and Raliv didn't want to be the bringer of sorrow.

Swinging by the farm store to get the cat food, he knew he couldn't help but be seen by the owner, who always called him by name, and always helped him find what he needed, although in truth, Raliv knew the store layout almost as well as he did. The store was bright and smelled of popcorn from the popcorn machine by the door that everyone helped themselves to. Men in overalls and work clothes wandered around, carrying plastic pipes and boxes of nails, and staring at the assortment of nuts and bolts, trying to find just the right size. Two women in jeans and sweatshirts were lingering by the seed display, comparing garden plans.

"Hi, Raliv," the shopkeeper said. "How are you doing?" It was a question about him, which in fact was a little different from the usual expressions of sympathy.

"I'm hanging in there, Fred. It's hard." Raliv surprised himself at the revelation, small and obvious as it was.

"I'm sure." Fred patted him familiarly on the shoulder. "What can I get for you?"

"I need a big bag of cat food, that kind Colleen always got." Raliv was searching for the brand name, but Fred had walked in his usual bouncy step towards the shelf and pulled down a bright white and red bag and was headed towards the counter.

Raliv paused by the seed display. Beans, squash, tomatoes, zucchini, broccoli. These would be essential for Colleen's garden. There was a basket of seed potatoes already showing their eyes and onion sets were tumbled into another basket. He was tempted, but maybe not yet. He still hadn't turned Colleen's garden patch from last year. He should do that first. But then he grabbed a packet of broccoli seeds. Those he needed to start inside.

At the counter, Fred was waiting patiently, smiling, not speaking. Raliv was moved by his lack of intrusion.

"What else, Raliv?"

"Get me a small bag of the potting soil out front."

"You got it."

"Hey, Fred. You got a minute? I want to show you something in my truck."

"Sure." Fred shoved an electronic pad before Raliv. Fred had opened a store account for Raliv and Colleen years ago. After Raliv had signed, Fred picked up the cat food and walked towards the door. Raliv had to hustle to keep up. Fred knew Raliv's old pickup and had already picked up the soil and placed both bags in the back by the time Raliv opened the passenger door and retrieved the rabbit pelt bag.

"Check this out." Raliv handed it to Fred. Fred turned it around in his hands, pressed it with his fingers.

"Wow, Raliv. Did you make this?" He looked up at Raliv.

"No. Someone gave it to me." Raliv wasn't sure why he was keeping the fact that they were intruders of a sort, someone poaching off his land, a secret. But he decided not to say more.

"It's beautiful. Someone really knows their stuff. Thanks for showing it to me." He handed the bag back to Raliv. "You take care." Fred hurried back in to take care of his store.

Raliv stood there a moment, inspecting the bag, then put the broccoli seeds in the bag, walked around, and climbed into his truck. At the Piggly Wiggly next door, he was painfully aware of the soft stares, the doe-eyed look of pity, even the occasional whisper between two shoppers as he passed.

This was so much harder to take than the simple asking of his well-being. This is what he had hoped to avoid. The simple truth was, he and Colleen had gone everywhere together. It was no doubt odd, still, seeing Raliv alone. As he loaded the plastic bags of his shopping into his truck cab, he thought about checking with the sheriff to see if he knew who this uninvited trapper on his land might be, but the idea of more human interaction convinced him to head home.

By the time Raliv got home, the sky had turned darker, and he could hear an occasional rumble of thunder off in the distance. He hurried to take in the groceries before it started to rain, then realized that if there was a note in the chair, it might get wet and be illegible, if he didn't hurry up and get it. And if there wasn't one there, Raliv could take comfort in knowing he had chased this person away.

He could carry the rest of the goods in later. Placing the milk and eggs in the refrigerator, he grabbed the note pad and pen he had used that morning and trotted out to the truck. He bounced through the field, through the opening in the rusty, sagging barbed wire fence, and over to the chair.

He glanced around, but no one was there. Or at least, he could see no one, but he had a feeling he was being watched again. A low grumble of thunder came. Raliv stopped close to the chair and climbed out of the truck.

On the seat of the chair was a piece of bamboo about fourteen inches long. He picked it up and saw that it had been made into a recorder. He put it to his mouth and blew, and a high-pitched whistle sounded. He put his fingers over the holes and blew again, raising his fingers at different intervals, changing the pitch.

He looked at the instrument again. He knew where the bamboo stand was growing in the bottoms, having cut cane fishing poles for the grandchildren there himself. But this was entirely different.

Then he remembered to look for the note. He reached into the gap where the note had been before and pulled out a tightly folded piece of paper, just as a large raindrop fell on his head. He gripped the recorder and the note and trotted back to the truck. By the time he closed the door, the rain started in.

He opened the note and read the block-lettered message:

21

```
I'm sorry for your loss. The ospreys
are nearly finished fixing up their nest
for this year. I hope you like the flute.
Maybe music can help fill the emptiness.
My name is not important. The less we
know, the more we name. I live here
right now.
```

Now, Raliv knew he had been being watched. Whoever it was, they had seen him looking at the aerie, seen him cry. He felt a little vulnerable, having been seen, but whoever it was, they were not being cold about it.

He looked up through the windshield at the osprey nest through the blur of rain. Over the years, the birds had added so many twigs and sticks, it was at least five feet across. And what did that even mean, "The less we know, the more we name?" And they live here now? Just who did they think they were?

Now the rain started pummeling the roof of the truck, making a low hum of drops on metal. Raliv put the recorder up to his mouth and tried playing different notes. Back when he was little, he had taken instruction on playing the instrument they called a Flutophone in grade school, but he didn't really recall what that entailed just now. It was the only music instruction he ever had, and his recollection of it was shrill whistles, as boys, ignoring the instruction from Ms Wiggington to blow softly, blew as hard as they could.

The cacophony of shrieks and mismatched notes was painful. Even then, Raliv had wondered what poor Ms Wiggington had done to someone to end up getting thirty second graders to play "Twinkle Twinkle Little Star" at an uneven pace. And it always ended with first his classmate Tommy, unable to keep himself from blowing as hard as he could, then every other boy on cue doing the same, and then about half the girls. Ms Wiggington would drop her arms in defeat.

Looking at the instrument again, he then realized he had

received two gifts now from whoever this was. He needed to give something back. He meant for them to leave, but returning a gift was only fair, even if they only took it and left.

He looked around his truck cab for something he could give and saw the groceries still on the floor. He had left some canned goods in the truck to take to the cabin. Pulling up the bag, he brought out two cans of sardines. If whoever this was had been living off of rabbits, maybe something different would taste good to them. And maybe they wouldn't take so many rabbits.

Raliv waited for the rain to abate before taking the cans over. He put the recorder back to his lips and struggled to find the notes at first, but finally played a halting, uneven opening of "Twinkle Twinkle Little Star."

He had to smile. What would Ms Wiggington think of that? The rain let up some and Raliv decided he had better hurry if he was going to get to the cabin. He put the recorder in his jacket pocket, picked up the notepad, and wrote quickly:

```
Thank you for my gifts. My name is
Raliv. Where did you come from? What
do you mean you live here? This is my
land. Who said you could live here? I
want to know your name.
```

He folded it up, then decided it would not survive the rain, so he retrieved a plastic baggy from the shopping bag and put the folded note inside and zipped it shut. He grabbed the two cans of sardines and ran over to the chair, hunching over to shield himself from the rain.

Wedging the note into the crevice, he placed the cans on the seat and trotted back to the truck. He drove back to the cabin to put away the staples he had bought, nearly getting stuck in the one large puddle at the head of the path. Unlocking the cabin, he went inside.

The rain came back in a deluge now, and he knew he would

need to stay at the cabin tonight. The road would be unpassable. The cat would be fine over night at the farmhouse. At least the rain barrels would be full. Tomorrow, after the rain stopped, he hoped, he would need to refill the water heater attached to the stove.

Shoving some old newspaper under the grate of the fireplace, he piled kindling atop and started the fireplace. He needed to dry himself out and warm up the damp air within the cabin. Once some larger pieces of wood started catching, he sat in his chair, watching the fire.

He welcomed the warmth. Watching the fire, he then recalled the little instrument in his jacket pocket. He got up and retrieved the piece and sat back at his chair. He kept playing the same little star song, over and over, hoping to get through it without a mistake.

He played very slowly, at first, focusing on getting just the right order. When he finally played it through without an error, albeit very slowly, he looked over at Colleen's chair and smiled. "Whatta ya think, Sweetie?"

He paused just a moment, as if waiting for a reply. Glancing out the window, he realized it had gotten dark. He turned back around and spoke to the chair again, "What should we have for supper?"

Getting up and opening the cabinet, he glanced around, then retrieved a can of soup that was closest to him. He dumped it into a small cast iron pot, placed the cover on, and put it just under the fire in the fireplace, then piled another log on top.

Colleen would have been snuggled into her chair, a big coverlet over her lap, with Felicity curled up on her. This is what he missed so much, the weave of their lives. Throughout their marriage, the past, the present, and the future had been the variables. And through it all, there were Raliv and Colleen, moving over and under time, creating that tight weave that was their world.

But now that fabric was rent. It was what made everything so hard, Raliv thought. All of their lifetime of experiences shared

Pan and the Message Chair

were changed. Their inside stories meant something precisely because they shared them. Someone would say something, maybe only using a particular word, that would bring back that shared memory, and they could share it again with only a glance across the room, and perhaps a gentle smile, while the person went on with whatever tale they had begun, completely oblivious to the second conversation that had just been had.

Alone, those intimate secrets simply meant nothing. And even if Raliv wanted to share that with someone else, one of their sons, or one of the few friends they had, it would never have the same meaning as it did to the two of them experiencing it together. It was only an anecdote. Those stories, those experiences, were lost, in a way. They were cherished as part of the weave. Now, they were mere recognition of what more was lost.

Raliv turned to Colleen's chair. "What was that song you and your sisters used to sing around the fire pit? Carter family song, remember?" He raised the recorder to his mouth and blew a couple of random notes, as if that might jar his memory. "Oh, I know. 'I never will marry.'"

He tried to pick out the tune. He found the first few notes, but he smelled the soup now and realized he was about to burn it. Putting the instrument down on the small table between the chairs, he grabbed an oven mitt from the hearth. He removed the lid and, in fact, the soup was boiling.

Sitting back in his chair, he ate the soup straight from the pan, burning his mouth on the first few bites, then put the pan and its lid directly into the fire, to burn off any residue. He poured a small glass of bourbon and sipped on it, as he watched the fire burn itself down to embers.

It had been a faster evening, playing the songs. He was glad for that. Standing and changing into his pajamas, he stared at the cozy bed he and Colleen had shared, but this time, instead of being sad, he caressed the memory of his life with Colleen.

"I love you," he whispered.

Then, he lay in the dark, trying to fall asleep.

Chapter 3
The Visitor

The visitor had known the old man was in the cabin, of course. He had smelled the smoke from the chimney for days now, carried low by the rain and humidity. He had seen him drive back on the narrow road in his rusty truck and had heard the pop of his rifle the day before.

As long as he stayed hidden, there was no reason for the visitor to ever be discovered. It was a farm that the owners appeared to have let deliberately stay wild around the edges, keeping it natural and relatively untended for their own pleasure. The visitor could not argue with that. It was the perfect spot to trap a few rabbits and rest up, before heading up into higher ground for the spring and summer months, up into the mountains, where a man can live peacefully enough and never disturb another person or be disturbed.

But he had not anticipated the old man climbing the hill first thing the next morning. The visitor had watched from behind a wide oak, his misshaped hat painted with wild grape juice and covered with brown oak leaves pulled low on his head.

His face and grey beard were blackened with charcoal from his campfire. His faded grey and black clothes and his natural, sinewy stature made him look like yet another tree in the woods. The sun was warm on his back. He expected the old man to pass by without a second glance. Crows called from down the hill in the woods.

The visitor was accustomed to people seeing right past him, whether he wanted them to or not, but just now, he definitely did not want to be seen. When the man tripped and fell, the visitor was preparing to stand away from the tree and be seen, although he worried about the gun he carried. It was a small bore but could do damage, nonetheless.

But if the old man was injured, he certainly could not leave him here alone. However, the older man was spryer than the visitor expected and righted himself. But he saw the snare. The visitor remained motionless.

The older man tromped on up the hill. He stopped at the top of the hill and looked up towards the sun, in a kind of silent prayer. The visitor understood now why the old man had come up. The visitor too was tired of the sour weather.

The visitor moved only his eyes, watching a decent sized rabbit that he had noticed earlier, that had been frightened by the old man's hike and tumble, now venturing forth again. The rabbit was moving away from the older man at the top of the hill and tripped the snare just as the old man squatted behind a stand of weeds.

The visitor rarely tried to hide by squatting. The way he saw it, it only made his bulk greater and more noticeable. No, he preferred to blend in by standing with the trees, motionless, and he often did so for hours if necessary.

Now, the older man was looking at the ground, as if to sit. The sprung snare was hardly more than an arm's reach away, and the visitor snatched the rabbit, along with the snare. Placing it behind his back, he reached behind himself and quickly twisted the rabbit's neck. Otherwise, he stayed in exactly the same spot.

The old man was looking right at him, but he did not even breathe, and the old man could not make him out. Now the old man was righting himself, looking down to gain his feet and, in that moment, the visitor stepped away, backwards, silently, subtly, until the old man began to turn.

Pan and the Message Chair

The visitor froze behind a different tree, much larger than the first. He watched the old man walk over to where he himself had been standing just seconds before, then look around himself, quizzically. The visitor realized he had perhaps underestimated this older man's abilities in the outdoors.

When the old man stomped down the hill, the visitor returned along the edge of the forest, down the long hillside to his camp. He walked inside the tree line, and if someone were to notice him, it would look like one of the trees was taking long strides down the hill.

The old man had not seen him, but he knew he was there, had seen both the snare and the rabbit caught in it. There was nothing else to do but try to get the old man to not turn him in, have the sheriff come and chase him off.

He didn't worry about being caught by the sheriff, since he could elude nearly anyone, especially if he made the mountains first. He just wasn't ready to move on yet. He had his little camp set up and didn't want to have to break it down so soon. And he needed to cure some meat for the trek.

His camp was simple enough, a debris shelter he had built under a root ball of a sycamore tree that stood atop a narrow ravine. He had placed a trash bag he found along the road up in the roots and filled out the sides with various pieces of deadfall, packing it with leaves and pine branches.

It was mostly dry inside, if a bit cramped for a man his size, but he made do. It was only temporary. Most people walking past would take no notice of the shelter; it looked more like a gathering of autumn's castoffs than a place to sleep. If he intended to stay, he would make a protected place for a small fire inside. As it was, when it wasn't pouring rain, he could only heat up stones and take them inside his shelter to keep him warm at night. But lately it had rained for days on end, and been chilly, so he had huddled in the shelter eating salted squirrel and smoked venison, wrapping himself in layers of faded, worn-out blankets.

After washing his face and hands of charcoal, he quickly skinned the rabbit near the creek that burbled below his little hut, then washed the cased pelt in the small stream. He strung the carcass over a tree limb with a woven stretch of rabbit leather. Then he went to his rucksack and pulled out his few possessions.

He figured if he paid for the rabbits he took, the old man could appreciate that and might let him stay. When he came to the little bag he had made from rabbit pelts, he decided that would do. Besides, he could replicate this work, so it wasn't as if it was something rare. He knew where he could leave the payment, but he also wanted to explain himself, at least a little bit, so the old man would not feel threatened.

The visitor listened to the breeze in the branches, heard the rustling of birds in the underbrush. Then he heard the truck on top of the ridge, spinning in a puddle. The visitor hurried. He pulled out an old envelope and froze for just a moment.

Inside was the letter, the one that had contained the news that had changed his life. He removed the letter carefully and put it back in his rucksack without reading it. He tore the envelope at the crease and used a small pencil from a miniature golf course to write the short note to the old man. He didn't want to say much, just reassure him that he was not in danger.

The visitor then strode quietly, but quickly, back up the hill. He followed a deer path, one he had taken a few times before, so he knew where the tripping hazards were. He reached the edge of the meadow just as the truck disappeared through an opening in the fallen-down fence.

Running quickly over to the big chair he had seen before, he placed the bag on the seat. He thought about putting the note in the bag, but seeing the notch in the seat of the chair, he decided it would be safer there, but only if the old man found it.

The visitor retreated to the edge of the woods and stood behind a stand of poplar trees to watch. The visitor let his surroundings engulf him. The sun was warm and welcome, shining on the swaying grasses in the field before him.

As he stood silently, a small deer walked past him, without seeing him. The deer stepped forward, grazed at some acorns from a red oak nearby, then moved on. Frogs croaked around the small pond near the chair. An osprey whistled high above him and sent its shadow across the clearing.

Then the truck came grumbling back towards him. It looked like he was driving past the chair, but then the truck stopped suddenly, and the man got out of the cab. The visitor saw him pick up the bag and look around. He looked right at the spot where the visitor stood, but he knew he could not discern him from the shadow of the trees. The old man retrieved the note too, now.

Good.

The visitor had had a chance to explain himself. Maybe that was enough.

Even when the old man drove off, the visitor stayed. He would stay until he smelled the old man's fire or until he saw the truck go by. If the old man stayed at the cabin, the visitor was safe. If he came back, it depended on what he did after that. If he drove straight back to his farmhouse, the visitor would leave. It likely meant he was calling the law on him.

It wasn't long before the visitor heard the truck coming back along the ridge again. He watched motionless as the man got out and walked over to the chair. The visitor could not decide just what he was doing.

The old man sat suddenly and looked out over the field. It was a good place to sit and enjoy a sunny spring day, the visitor agreed, but then the old man raised his arm towards an osprey flying overhead and yelled, "Look."

The old man dissolved into tears. The visitor watched the old man weep. This man was suffering deeply, the visitor knew. And the visitor knew what it was like to suffer. He was tempted to leave the man in peace, but moving meant taking the risk of being seen. The old man's sorrow was palpable, and the visitor felt his own eyes water just watching the man's grief, for that was clearly what it was: grief. That was the only feeling that could have suddenly gripped that old man.

Then he stopped crying, looking exhausted. The visitor

watched him move away, then turn and put a piece of paper on the chair seat, then leave.

When he was certain the old man and his truck were gone, the visitor went to the chair and retrieved the note that had been left for him. It meant the old man probably wasn't going to call the sheriff on him. The visitor strode down the hillside as the afternoon began to wane. He built a small fire next to the creek and skewered the rabbit meat and propped it up over the flames.

On a separate stick, he propped his thready, stained socks on the other side of the fire to dry them from all the walking through the wet forest during the day. Whatever the old man's grief was, it made the visitor sorry to see. There was nothing more human than grief, but that did not make it any less painful to go through.

He sat quietly for a long time, until the rabbit was cooked through. He watched the flames of his small campfire, ate half the meat, and strung the rest up in the sycamore, and he remembered. He remembered his own grief, that never truly went away, but eventually became a part of him that he could learn to live with. It was as if he had grown some hideous third arm that never helped in any way, but he could work around it now.

An owl called from a nearby tree and was answered from another farther downstream. Tree frogs brought the forest full of a repeated "ree-ree-ree." The visitor had once been like the old man. In some ways, maybe, they chose the same path as a result. But the visitor wasn't certain he would wish his path on anyone else, wasn't certain he himself would choose the same path again.

When the flames had died down, the visitor banked the coals against a large stone he had used for part of his fire pit and picked up one of the other stones with a sooty, scratchy blanket and moved it to his shelter. He curled up next to the warm rock, covered himself with blankets and leaves, and slept with the chorus of night sounds and a backdrop of the trickling stream.

The visitor was awakened by the snap of a twig a few yards

away from him. He heard a sweeping sound, then a pause, then another sweeping sound. It had to be a deer, rummaging through the leaves for acorns.

Something about sleeping helped the visitor know just what he wanted to share with the old man. It was the only thing that had made his own life bearable, or as bearable as it was: music. Maybe music could help the old man express himself, express his pain, and work through it, the way he himself had. He knew it might not help. Maybe the old man needed to write, or to draw, but maybe it was music, and the visitor had to try. He could replicate the recorder. He had built several over the years, and he had seen bamboo growing along the creek bed near a beaver pond.

He pulled his little flute out of his pack and looked again at the note the old man had left him. Why do people think a name is so important, he wondered. A name is just a construct parents give their children, a tool for telling them how to behave, how to grow up, how to live. But parents can only know how they themselves should behave, how they themselves should choose. Children inevitably learn what they need to know to live their own lives, and names have little to do with it.

And then there was the part in the note about private property. Did the old man tell the osprey to move on? Did he yell at the owls that they were trespassing? Of course not, because they are wild. And the visitor considered himself just as wild as the animals the old man seemed to welcome. Why shouldn't the visitor be just as welcome?

He climbed out of the shelter and looked around him and the deer bounded off over the hill. He looked up at the sky and saw it was threatening rain again and scowled. All this rain made catching rabbits or squirrels very hard, and it made watching for them cold and miserable work.

Lowering the rest of the rabbit down, he gnawed the meat off the tough carcass. He put the bones in his battered aluminum pot and filled it with creek water and placed it next to the fire pit. If nothing else, he could have broth from the marrow tonight, assuming he had time to make a fire before the rain began. But he had things to do this morning, and he would not leave a fire unattended, even one as small as he generally made.

He would have liked to have aired out his blankets but didn't want them rained on. Instead, he made his way along the creek bed to where the bamboo stand grew. He took his camp knife from its sheath and cut one stalk, then cut it again about a foot and a half long. That gave him room to carve.

He was looking forward to making a new recorder and thought maybe this time he would make some engravings along the side, just for decoration. He spent a great deal of time whittling and carving, so a few scratches on the bamboo would not be difficult. Maybe he would carve an osprey in flight along the side. That way, he would recall where he had made it.

Returning to his camp, he started the fire for his broth. He put the pan next to the small flame and went to his rucksack where he pulled out the scrap of paper left from the envelope and wrote a note to the old man.

He wanted to say he understood what the old man was going through, even if his particular grief was unique to him. It was true, telling him he was sorry for the loss meant giving away that he had been watching, but the way the old man looked around him, he had already sensed it, the visitor knew.

Then he wrote the part about the ospreys finishing their nest. It was clearly important to the old man, and the visitor wanted to share with him that success. Maybe it would cheer the old man some to know the birds were safe.

While the water boiled, he worked on the new recorder, carving holes and making a mouthpiece from a bit of a maple branch that had fallen on the forest floor. Then he decided it was time to leave his gift. The visitor dowsed the fire with sand from the bank of the creek, then traipsed back along the game trail to the chair.

He listened for the truck, and when he didn't hear it, he strode over to the chair and left the flute and the note. Retreating to the woods, he waited for the old man to return. He was worried the rain might come first and make his note unreadable. The clouds were dark and low now.

Standing motionless, he listened to the redwings call and the trees creaking limb against limb in wind. The grasses in the meadow were bent over now, flattened by the wind. It promised to be a strong rain. His broth would be even more watery than normal, but he stayed.

Then he heard the grumble of the truck coming along the dirt road from the farmhouse. The first few drops of rain landed on the visitor's clothes. He did not move. Trees do not duck out of the rain: they stand up to it and drink it in.

The old man stopped the truck and went over to the chair. He picked up the recorder and the note, then looked around himself, looking for the visitor, of course. He did not move. Then, as the rain began in earnest, the old man trotted back to his truck and climbed in.

The rain poured down. It was cold and penetrating, but the visitor did not move. Then he heard muffled flute playing in the truck, and he managed a smile. The old man opened the truck door and ran back over to the chair, leaving something shiny there, then ran back to the truck and left. It was a deluge now.

When the sound of the truck had faded, the visitor stepped out into the field, his grey clothes barely perceptible in the grey rain. He retrieved the note in the bag and the two cans of sardines. His mouth watered. Sardines. It would not be watery broth tonight.

He didn't take the note out of the plastic in the rain. There would be time for that in his hut. Turning, he made his way to the tree line in the pouring rain, then wended his way down to his camp. He was drenched. He stripped off his clothes and hung them on various twigs in his shelter and wrapped himself in blankets.

Then he sat in his cramped shelter and read the note. He liked the old man's name: Raliv. It fit, somehow. But he still wasn't happy with the visitor's presence. There was still work to do on that account. The visitor hunched in his hut, played a soft tune on his recorder, then ate a tin of sardines. It tasted like a feast. Food. Maybe he could share his food with Raliv. Everyone eats.

That was it, something he knew Raliv could use. It grew dark early in the rain and the visitor curled up and slept.

Chapter 4
Raliv

The next day came cloudy, but dry and warmer. Raliv was up early, making the strong coffee he preferred. It was oats again today. There was not a lot of variety to choose from, since they really only kept canned goods and some rice, oats, and beans in big plastic bins, but in fact, Raliv just didn't care.

He was eating to stay alive. Wasn't that "taking care of himself," as people urged? He put on his jacket and sat at the picnic table again, this time facing the table so he could rest the hot bowl of oats on the tabletop and watch the woods around him.

He liked living in the woods with nature surrounding him. He fed the birds and watched for the other animals whose world he now inhabited. He followed with his eyes as a flock of a dozen or more robins hopped up the bosky hill through the dried leaves. Separately, randomly, they hopped, flipped over a few leaves, hopped again, flipped some leaves, in a haphazard dance of birds and leaves. They were all spread out over thirty square yards or so.

Raliv watched them make their way up the hill, looking like raindrops on a pond, except birds in the leaves. It was a dance with no sound. They crossed over the hilltop and made their way beyond his sight. He took another bite. He heard one of the ospreys give its chirping whistle somewhere far above him. He looked up to try to find it, but it was out of sight, hidden in the leafless web of tree branches above him. A downy woodpecker darted from a tree trunk to a hollow spar farther up the hillside, then gave it a quick, battering beat, a pause, another battering beat, another battering beat.

The air was still. The forest was full of tweets and rustlings of animals, but no breathing of trees in the breeze. Raliv let his mind wander to this strange visitor on his land. Who was this person? What did he want? Or she? He really had no way of knowing.

Raliv ate his cereal slowly, it was pretty much flavorless, but he ate it anyway. He wondered what he might find at the chair today. Then he decided he needed to be ready to leave something this time, instead of relying on whatever was handy. But what would they want? What would they need? He had no way of knowing, not knowing anything about them.

As he gulped down his last bit of coffee, getting a few unwelcome grounds in his mouth, he realized what he should give them: string. They had used shoelaces for their snare. String would be better, and Raliv had a whole ball of string in the cabin. In fact, he had numerous balls of string in the farmhouse he had gathered, to have his students make homemade Newton's cradles using hot glue guns and marbles back when he taught conservation of energy. String. He had lots of it, just like he had lots of rabbits, he supposed.

He took his cup and bowl into the house and cleaned them, then rummaged around in the desk until he found the ball of twine. Did he want to encourage the poaching? It seemed illogical. Still, he did in fact have lots of rabbits on the farm, and whoever this was did not seem malicious, but then, how would he know, beyond his own gut feeling on it?

He took the string and shoved it into his jacket pocket with the notepad and pen and headed for the door. Just before he reached the door, he remembered the recorder and went over to the little table beside his overstuffed chair and retrieved it. He locked the door again, but somehow, it didn't really seem necessary.

Climbing into the truck, he drove the path through the woods. It was still muddy, but passable. He watched a rabbit dart up the path ahead of him, stopping for a moment to look at the truck bouncing awkwardly towards him, then dash off to the side. Yeah, Raliv had plenty of rabbits.

By the time he reached the chair, Raliv found he was a little nervous, eager. He stopped the truck, turned off the motor, and jumped out of the cab. There was something there, alright. Something green, maybe, on the chair.

Raliv checked his pocket to make sure he had the string. He went over to the chair and picked up the baggie he had left the note in the day before. It was filled with green leaves. He opened the baggie.

Wild arugula.

Raliv loved arugula. He and Colleen had often foraged for it on the farm and had even sown the seeds after they found some that had already bolted in the summer heat. Raliv tried to recall when he had last eaten a salad. This would be delicious. He eyed the bag for a moment, then put the open bag to his nose and smelled deeply. It was a fresh, grassy, peppery scent. His stomach gave a slight growl.

Then, he felt into the crevice of the chair and pulled out the folded-up piece of paper. The paper was very small, and the lettering was so tiny, Raliv could barely make it out:

```
    Thank you for the fish. They were
very good. I don't get fish very often.
I like your name. It is different. I
myself have many names. It depends on
who is doing the naming. Yes, you do
own the land. So do the osprey and the
rabbit. I will not harm the land.
```

Raliv paused a moment. He had to agree that while it was true that only Raliv and Colleen paid taxes on the land, he certainly felt that the animals and the trees and flowers and all of it belonged to the land, and the land to them.

He traced the tree line to see if he was being watched. He was certain he was. He could feel it. But all he could see beyond the drooping tops of the Johnson grass was the long line of grey-black tree trunks, punctuated by the occasional juniper tree, scraggly evergreens with tops that sagged to one side in the stillness of the day. He saw no one. Sitting at the chair, he pulled out the string and put it next to him on the seat. Then he pulled out the notepad and pen and wrote in careful letters:

```
    No, I don't think you will harm
the land. I do think the land belongs
to what lives here, but are you sure
that includes you? You have to respect
people's privacy, you know. I appreciate
the arugula. Colleen and I love it.
```

Raliv thought about whether he should correct the note, since Colleen was gone, but decided she was, very much, still part of his life these days, and somehow, crossing her name off would seem to dishonor her, a further, painful acknowledgement of her being gone too soon. He folded up the piece of paper and wedged it onto the little gap in the seat.

Taking his bag of arugula, he returned to his truck. He drove over to the farmhouse to take care of Felicity. When he walked into the kitchen, he took off his boots and hung his jacket on the peg by the backdoor. Then he remembered the recorder and took it out of the jacket and placed it and the bag of arugula on the maple table, where he saw all the groceries he had not put away yesterday still sitting there.

He wondered if Felicity had investigated them. She was pretty good at staying off the table when he was around, lest she get a sharp rebuke from Raliv, which always sent her scurrying as if surprised he still lived in the house. He did not like the idea of her on his table, but he was pretty certain she knew when he was away and took every liberty she chose then.

He was putting away the canned vegetables in the cupboard when John, his son, rushed through the kitchen door. John stopped, looking a bit breathless, and looked at Raliv intently for a second.

"Well, do come in, Son." Raliv placed a can of cream-style corn on the shelf.

"Dad!" John started taking off his coat, too heavy for these temperatures, thought Raliv.

"Who else did you expect?"

"Where have you been?"

"What?" Raliv turned now and straightened up. "Right here." He shrugged. John picked up a plastic bag filled with canned condensed soups and carried them over to Raliv.

"But Dad, I've been calling and calling, and you never answer." He handed the bag to Raliv.

"Oh, that." Raliv took the bag and turned back to the cupboard. "I've been out at the cabin."

John shrugged. "Jeez, Dad. Why do you go out there and sit all alone like that? That can't be healthy." John turned around and looked at the table. "I don't even know why you have that old shack anyway."

"I'm not alone out there." Raliv folded up the plastic bag and shoved it into the sleeve where they kept them … where he kept them, now … for reuse. Yes, he was talking about the birds and trees and all the animals in the woods, but he also realized suddenly he was talking about the rabbit bag person. He ran the idea through his thoughts for a moment. He wasn't alone on the farm after all.

John had been attentive to Raliv's well-being over the last few months, calling on him and checking on him. He had brought his children to visit Colleen one last time when she was so ill, and he had returned later to buy groceries and fix meals for Raliv, who had somehow forgotten to eat for four months.

Raliv was just glad he was here.

"Yeah, I know, Pop." John pulled out a chair from next to the table and sat familiarly. "You love your nature and all, but really, in these times? Why can't you at least take a cell phone with you? You still have Colleen's, right?" John looked up hopefully. Raliv put a cardboard box of cherry tomatoes on the counter next to the refrigerator and put the cucumber and carrots in the crisper. He placed some bright oranges and tangerines in a bowl on the table. He always had difficulty passing up the brightness of citrus fruits. After putting the three apples he had bought in another bowl, he slid both bowls onto the counter. It was true, he had a phone, or rather Colleen had had one, since they didn't see the need for two phones when they themselves were always together.

Raliv smiled and pulled out another chair and sat across from John. The living room was far more comfortable than these cane-bottomed chairs, but somehow, this is where they always sat - in the kitchen. "There's no signal out there anyway, John. Remember?"

John smiled now too, no doubt recalling his own frustration at being at the cabin with Raliv and Colleen and being so out of touch with his business world and expressing it vocally to his parents. "Dad, you know you can come and stay with us. I worry about you. I don't want you to be lonely, and this sure seems like a recipe for lonely."

"And take whose bedroom, John? JJ's? I couldn't sleep with that poster on his wall." Raliv tried to chuckle, but it was hard to, for some reason. "Or Becky? A girl has to have her room to run to, you know that." Raliv placed his hands, palm open and turned up, on the table.

"Yes, and slam the door." John nodded but still managed a smile. "We could figure it out. You know that. And the kids would love to have you there, and Tina too. She's worried about you too."

"Yeah, I know we could figure it out. And maybe at some

point. But it's too soon to do that, ohn. I really do appreciate it. I know you're thinking about me, but I have to do this on my own schedule, you know?" Raliv shifted his weight in his chair, the cane creaking slightly. He looked down to see if it needed repair. He was constantly looking for things to repair these days. The seat was fine.

"What's this?" Raliv looked up and John was holding the recorder.

"Oh, that's just a present someone gave me." Raliv felt like snatching it from John's hands, but he wasn't damaging it. Still, he resisted a strong urge. John put the instrument to his mouth and gave it a shrill blast, blowing far too hard. Now Raliv did reach for it, but still resisted the urge to grab at it.

John put it back down on the table, dropping it the last couple of inches. "Where did you get this, Dad? Is it homemade? It's nice."

Raliv stood suddenly and picked up the recorder. It wasn't at all damaged, but he didn't like it being dropped like that. He felt a little like a petulant child, hoarding his simple treasure. "I told you, a friend gave it to me." We walked over and put the recorder in his jacket. "And yes, it is homemade. And nicely done, I might add."

He turned over the phrase in his head a few times: a friend.

"A friend?" John's eyes were wider now with curiosity.

Raliv turned and faced John. "Yeah, a friend. I do have friends, you know."

"I know, Pop. Sorry. I'm glad you do." Now he was eyeing the bag of arugula. Raliv picked it up and put it into the refrigerator. He didn't know why he was keeping this visitor to the farm a secret, but somehow, it seemed better that way. John would be worried about Raliv's safety, no doubt, and maybe Raliv should too, but he didn't feel at all threatened. He sometimes worried that his sons thought of him only as a fusty old man, unable to care for himself. "Can I get you anything, Dad? Anything I can do?" Raliv knew this was the start of John's having to leave.

"No, John. I think I'm okay. Thank you for coming by. I'm

sorry I worried you."

"Oh, it's just me, I think." He stood and looked at Raliv. "I miss her too, Dad."

"I know, Son." Raliv reached out and pulled John in for a long hug. He always thought of John and Brian as their sons, but in fact, she was their stepmother, although she had given them the warmth and love of a second mother, without ever trying to replace their birth mother. He knew her death was hard on them as well, and the grandchildren.

John left, promising to call on the weekend, although in fact, Raliv didn't always know what day of the week it was, having no work regimen to remind him these days. And Raliv promised to charge up the phone and to start carrying it with him, even if there wasn't always a signal.

After John had left, Raliv tried to think of what to have with his arugula. He wanted to eat it while it was still fresh, and a can of soup or a dollop of beans hardly seemed worthy. He looked over at Colleen's chair. What would she want? "I know." Raliv raised a finger in recognition of his thought. "I'll fix that chicken dish you like."

He caught himself up short and almost corrected himself aloud. "Used to like" would have been the words, but it was enough to think them, and his mood sullened. He went over to the freezer and removed a small bag of chicken to thaw. There should still be time to thaw it, he thought. Placing the bag in the sink, he then returned to the fridge. He fought off the dark mood.

He looked back at Colleen's chair. "What else is in that dish, honey?" Opening the refrigerator door again, he peered in. He pulled out bottles and jars and checked their fullness, then rechecked the expiration dates. He had what he needed. Good. He was set. He pulled his head out and put the lemon juice back in. It was too early to take things out, but he was glad to know he had what he wanted. He knew he had flour and seasonings.

Closing the refrigerator, he put his hands on his hips. What should he do now? It was early yet, but he had no chores. He had fixed everything that was broken. The house was spotless from his compulsive cleaning when he ran out of other tasks. Then he remembered the broccoli seeds he had bought. It took him a moment to recall he had left the seeds in the rabbit bag in the truck. That's what he could do. He could start the broccoli.

Raliv went out to the truck and got the soil from the back and the seeds from the front. He carried them to the back porch, to a low row of shelves Raliv had built for Colleen to use as her potting area. Then he went inside and retrieved the cardboard egg cartons they had saved for just this purpose. He cut the tops off the egg cartons then cut open the potting soil and scooped out enough to fill two trays and dropped several seeds into each egg spot. That would be plenty of broccoli, he decided.

He carried them in gently and put them in the kitchen window. That felt good, he decided, to get those started. He looked over the little rows of dirt, sprinkled them with enough water to moisten them good, then turned to the table again.

"I guess I really need to turn the garden tomorrow, don't I, Honey? Put the compost in. Or maybe it's too soon. Don't want to dry it out." He stared at the chair, but his focus blurred. John was right, of course. Raliv really didn't have what he would call close friends around here. This was Colleen's hometown, not his. And this was her family farm she had inherited, and now he inherited.

He wasn't aloof or distant with people, he didn't think. It was just that Colleen was his best friend and she had filled his world, their world. He did have good friends, but they were from before, from youth, even. He stayed in touch with them and got together for an occasional lunch in his hometown some two hours away, but here, he didn't know whom he would ever rely on if he had to.

He didn't want to dwell on it. He decided he needed to turn the compost pile that minute. Hurrying about, he put on his boots and pulled out his split-leather work gloves. Staying busy helped keep him from going to the depths of sorrow he struggled against. Out at the shed, he pulled out the spade and turned to the compost pile beside the old barn, trying hard to focus on the task at hand. Before he put away the shovel, he hosed off the steel blade. Then he sat in a lawn chair, just to catch his breath, and an image he had been trying to avoid for weeks overtook him.

He returned to a memory of Colleen, looking gaunt and tired from the treatments, saying a bit angrily that the doctors were pumping her full of poison and she didn't want that. She knew intuitively very early on what the outcome was going to be. But Raliv had urged her to try. If Raliv had hope, perhaps that was wrong, but he couldn't see even now why that was wrong. Had he been selfish to try to save his Colleen? Perhaps now, it seemed so. But if he had not tried, if he had done nothing, she would still be gone, and he was not sure he could live with himself now if he had not tried everything he could to save her.

And he had.

They had tried. But recalling how bad she felt was still an image he could not stand to bring up. He wanted to remember the good years, and there was so much more of that: the travels, the nights on the back porch together, the dancing in the kitchen to their favorite songs. Why did the dark, sick time have to be so damned vivid? There was too much to celebrate to let the darkness win. Somehow, recognizing that had he not tried he would forever wonder "what if?" That would have been unbearable, made him feel a little less guilty. They had, after all, made the best decisions they could. Everything else was sorrow masquerading as regret. Even coming to these terms, and the meager solace they provided, Raliv let himself weep again. Sitting in the webbed chair, he cried it out for a long time, because he missed her so.

Finally, Raliv wiped his cheeks, took a deep breath, and went in to clean up. Felicity ran from room to room with him, glad to have the companionship. Every time he stood from a chair, she would gallop in front of him, then fall over and stretch out for him to pet her side, which he did just about every time, being the well-trained human in the relationship.

Pan and the Message Chair

He decided to wait on cooking supper. If he ate too early, he would be hungry again before bedtime. He sat in the living room of their farmhouse, trying to decide if he wanted to watch television. He and Colleen had programs they enjoyed together but it just wasn't the same alone. It wasn't that he hated doing what they had done together because it made him sad again, necessarily, but that the programs simply weren't as enjoyable now. Raliv looked at the mantle clock. It probably was time for the local news. Maybe he should see what was going on in the world. Perhaps that would make him less focused inwards.

The television lit up the room, and the newscaster, a somber gray-haired man, in a suit and tie, told about a war in Asia, an outbreak of a disease in Europe, and political gridlock and bickering in the United States. He was about to turn the television off, disgusted with the prospect of more bad news, when the weather came on. The young woman was bright and enthusiastic and was eagerly forecasting an unexpected cold blast coming later in the week. She was very excited about the prospect of snow on Saturday.

In fact, snow was not uncommon around here in March, thought Raliv. Some of their heaviest snows sometimes occurred in March. But then he thought about the rabbit bag person. Where were they sleeping? Could they find shelter from the cold? They certainly seemed resourceful. Still, if it was going to be as cold as the forecaster said, all the way down to the teens, he found himself worrying. Perhaps he could leave one of his old parkas at the chair for them. Although, with temperatures in the teens, who knew if that was enough? He decided to figure out the best way to help them, somehow. After all, they had given him dinner, or at least part of it. And the recorder.

He looked at the clock again. It was still earlier than he ordinarily would eat, but the idea of cooking enticed him. He went into the kitchen and flattened out the chicken, although it was still a bit frozen. But the thinning out would help it defrost. He tossed the arugula with some diced cucumber and some split cherry tomatoes, poured some olive oil on top, then dripped some lemon juice on it. He ground some pepper on top, tossed on some kosher salt from the salt well next to the stove, and put it aside. Then he cooked the chicken piccata.

It came together quickly and Raliv was excited to be eating something more varied from his usual menu of canned goods and unadorned game from the cabin. He got out one of Colleen's favorite plates, a bright yellow and blue dish they had picked up in Santa Fe on one of their trips west. Pullling a placemat from the drawer and a matching cloth napkin, he set the table with a knife and fork. He poured the last bit of the sauvignon blanc into a wine glass and set the full dinnerplate down. He stood at his chair and surveyed the scene.

Colleen would be proud of me, he decided. Towards the end, when she was very weak, she had told him it would be hard on him, but that she wanted him to try to move on. But no one moves on from a love like they had. One learns, over time, to find his footing maybe, to navigate in a different world than the one he had built with Colleen, if he is lucky. And although Raliv wasn't there yet, he had very consciously told himself, "I need to choose to seek happiness," even if he did not see where that would come from just now.

After Raliv had eaten and cleaned up, he retired to the living room. This time, instead of bourbon, he had opened a bottle of cabernet and took a glassful with him to the table next to the overstuffed chair. He brought the recorder with him, and after he had sat and Felicity had settled in on his lap, he played. First there was "Twinkle Twinkle," then he started on "Amazing Grace." The other song he had started earlier had been harder than he was ready for. He played the old hymn over and over, to try to remember the fingering from one time to the next, which wasn't all that complicated. Finally, after he had made it through the song successfully and had finished half the glass of wine, he looked over at Colleen's chair. She would have liked to hear him play. He imagined her sitting there, listening, maybe knitting.

"So, how do you like my playing?" Raliv asked her chair. "Not too bad, huh?" Felicity opened one eye and looked up at him, then closed her eye again and snuggled her head into his lap. "I got this from the rabbit bag person, remember?" He held the recorder up into the line of vision had she been sitting there, then looked back down at the calico. "I don't know their name, though. Just some woodland fellow." He paused, then looked up and smiled. "Maybe I'll call him 'Pan.' It would make sense, right? Woodland? Flute?" Then he laughed, for the first time in a long time, at the prospect of naming this person, whoever they were, after the mythological creature.

Chapter 5

Raliv was awakened the next morning by Felicity walking the length of his body from his ankles to his chest, then stopping to smell his breath while purring loudly in his face.

"Okay, must be time to get up, huh, Felicity?" He was maybe a little miffed at being awakened from his sleep earlier than he would have ordinarily gotten up, but he couldn't be angry at the cat for just being a cat. He sat up and Felicity jumped off. He looked at the clock, although he had no place he needed to be especially. It was only a half hour earlier than his normal rising time. No problem. He had slept well that night.

After going through his morning routine in the bathroom, Felicity deciding that was the best time to enjoy her own breakfast from the gravity feeder next to the sink, Raliv dressed and made his way into the kitchen. It was almost muscle memory to go make coffee and clean the countertops, but instead, he remembered something he had not thought of in a long time.

Several years before, he and Colleen had bought a small home espresso machine on a whim at a specialty shop in the city. They had enjoyed it on and off for a good bit, but then, in one of Colleen's frustrated efforts to create more counter space, it had been put on a shelf in the closet, easy to retrieve whenever they wanted to make a cup, and promptly forgotten.

He pulled the machine out now and put it next to a plug on

the counter. Locating the grinder in the pantry, he fished around in the coffee bin until he found the whole bean espresso roast. He worried it might be too old, but decided he had nothing to lose. After he had filled the machine, he turned it on to let it work. It was not a quick brewing process, so he busied himself getting the milk out and heating up a small cast iron skillet for an egg. He poured some milk into a small metal cup, ready to heat with the steam. He was ready to break the egg into the warming frying pan when he decided he would make a recipe from his childhood, and from his own sons', "Eggs with a Hat," although it seemed every family had a special name for it. He had just bought some bread yesterday. Why not?

He got the bread out and a small juice glass, cut a circle out of a slice of bread and tossed it into the skillet he had already coated with a little olive oil. He let it cook for a moment, then flipped both the bread and the circle, broke the egg into the center, and went to check on the now-hissing espresso maker. He turned the lever on the machine to froth the milk, the steam gurgling through. After pouring his espresso, he added the heated milk, then flipped the egg. He always drank his regular coffee black, but he liked his espresso with a little milk and a spoonful of sugar.

When he had doctored his coffee and plated his egg, he sat at the table to eat his breakfast. The scent of the coffee, the frying egg, and toasting bread made him recall one of the trips to Paris he and Colleen had had. They had traveled the world together, but always came back to their little farmhouse and the cabin at the back of the farm. It was such a contrast, he knew. Back at the cabin, which Colleen had suggested they build as a place for them to just retreat from the bother of the world, everything was simple, primitive, safe. But then they ventured far out into the world, just the two of them, over and over.

They had been to Paris at least a dozen times. It was their favorite city. If they planned a trip to Barcelona, they included several nights in Paris. If they went to Bruges, they also went to Paris. There was one area where they had stayed several times, around the rue Cler, where they knew the shops and restaurants, although over the years, some had changed ownership and some had even gone out of business.

Near the corner of rue Cler and rue de Grenelle, they had been staying in the coarse little Hotel La Serre overlooking the street market, which opened noisily each day early, the clanging of stanchions and clunking of wooden crates awakening them to the pungent and exotic odor of the fromagerie below. One morning, they discovered a bakery, a boulangerie, there around the corner, where they served a delicious and inexpensive breakfast of fried eggs, sautéed salty ham, orange juice, espresso, and pieces of the wonderful baguettes. He and Colleen loved it and went there just about every morning while they were in the area, eating the hearty food and watching the people pass by the window, where a few tables had been crammed into the back of the shop.

They stood in the same line as those buying their daily loaf of bread or a beautiful sweet bread from the case, paid, then sat in the back, waiting. The woman who ran the breakfast part stayed busy, then looked up at whosever order was ready and said in a very normal volume, "Petit-déjeuner," and handed the plates over the orange squeezer to their outstretched hands. In the shop and in the street, people lined up to buy a loaf of bread, the queue moving quickly and efficiently as locals and tourists waited patiently.

They had been saddened to find on one trip that the bakery was gone, and a clothing store had opened up instead. It was funny how a smell could take him back immediately to a memory. But unlike some times recently, he found he could revel in this one now.

He embraced the image of Colleen, her scarf she just bought the day before at the flower market on Île de la Cité around her neck in the chill of the spring morning, smiling and watching Parisians walking to school or the office with their satchels and briefcases. Or maybe they carried their shopping bags to the green grocer across the street, the stall filled with myriad colors of wonderful produce. The look of sheer delight in being able to share that morning with the people of Paris covered Colleen's face. Raliv spent as much time watching her enjoying herself as he did watching the passersby. And in the background, the hissing of the coffee machine, the clanging of great pans full of pastries, and the smell of the bread, the coffee, and the eggs. Then he ate his breakfast, imagining the two of them in Paris again. The espresso was perfect.

Once he had cleaned up after breakfast, Raliv got out his pad and a pen to write down what he had on his list today. He sat at the kitchen table to write but could think of nothing he needed to do. He looked out the backdoor window. It was a grey sky, but bright. Had he really done so much he had no chores left? The prospect should have made him happy, he supposed, but it instead frustrated him a bit. What was he going to do if he had nothing to cross off his list?

He didn't want to sit all day and brood. He knew he wanted to go by the chair, but that didn't seem like something to put on a to-do list. It was still mid-morning, so he had all day. Maybe he could go by the chair earlier than he usually did. He was still looking at the blank paper, fingering the pen, waiting for a task to come to mind that he could write down. If he went by early, he might catch a glimpse of Pan. He smiled to himself at the name. He definitely wanted to share the name with his new friend.

Raliv looked up and out the kitchen window. He set his mouth in a thin line. "His new friend" was an interesting thought. Was this person a friend? He knew nothing about them. They certainly seemed to know more about him, being able to spy on him at will, it seemed. Or maybe it was only when Raliv was at the chair that they spied on him.

It was true, he had a definite sense of being watched at the chair that he did not have here at the farmhouse or at the cabin. Maybe they only stayed around the pasture near the pond. But they had been to the bamboo patch down in the bottoms, evidently.

Raliv looked around himself now. Where was the recorder?

Pan and the Message Chair

He stood and walked into the living room. It was there on the small table between their chairs where he had left it. He picked it up and put it in his shirt pocket, although it was too long to leave there for long, the bamboo reaching up to his jaw. Still he liked having it there, close. He returned to the kitchen and sat back down. The recorder scraped his chin as he sat, so he took it out of his pocket and put it on the table. What could he leave for Pan today?

Raliv liked giving practical gifts that people might not get for themselves but that they might later say, "Thanks for that pressure cooker. I use it all the time." Funny, Pan had given him more frivolous things: a rabbit skin bag, a flute, and even arugula was more a luxury than a necessity. But what in the world would this person he knew nothing about need or want? Did they need a blanket? There was the cold snap coming. Could they use a tarp? Raliv had a whole collection of tarps of various sizes he had managed to acquire over the years, far more than he could ever find a use for. What was it about a tarp that just seemed so wonderfully practical, even if you had no use for it?

Since he evidently had all day to do it, he decided he would simply ask Pan what he might need. What was so difficult about that? He would stop by the chair on the way to the cabin and simply ask what Pan might need and then he could go and fill up the water heater attached to the woodstove. He had meant to do that before. Then when he went back by, he could check the chair again to see what Pan needed. He started to write it down as part of his list, but he surely didn't need a list with only one thing on it.

Putting on his jacket, he grabbed the pad, then headed towards the door. But then he stopped, remembering the recorder. He retrieved the instrument from the table and went out the back door to bring the rabbit bag inside. He suddenly had a bad feeling about it being taken by a raccoon or some other creature from the potting shelves out back.

He hung the bag on the key hook and the weight caused the small piece of wood that held the hooks to flop off the wall.

He put it back up, the screws only tenuously holding into the stripped-out hole in the drywall. That was something he could fix later. He found he was a bit glad for that, for something to repair.

He started to head for the door again, but then he remembered his promise to carry the cell phone. He knew where it was - still sitting on the bedside table on Colleen's side of the bed. He checked the battery. Not fully charged, but okay until he could recharge it later that night when he returned. No, he wouldn't be able to make or receive phone calls from the cabin, but sometimes he could get and send messages. John was right. He was glad to have it in his pocket.

Now he went to his truck. Outside, it was warm and breezy. Raliv could see a blue line where the clouds were blowing away, far up on the horizon. The truck grumbled to life after grinding several times. Then he drove past the catalpa tree and through the opening in the busted barbed-wire fence towards the stump-become-chair-become-mailbox.

He stopped farther away from the chair this time. He didn't want to crush any of the other bulbs that were now sending up new small green shoots. The tall grasses of the pasture itself were bowing and flowing as if a river current ran through them. A red-winged blackbird gave out a "conk-a-lee" from the other side of the pond. At first, Raliv didn't see anything on the chair and decided maybe he was too early. He took the pad and pen and walked towards the chair. Then he saw there was something there: a rock. Well, talk about something frivolous; what kind of gift was that? A rock?

But when he reached the chair and picked it up and looked at it, he saw that it was in fact a geode that had been broken open, the crystal side facing down on the seat of the chair. It was beautiful. The geode itself was about the size of his palm, and the perfectly formed crystals were a pale purple. He had seen plenty of geodes in his life, but this one was unusual in the clarity of the crystals. If he had geodes of any sort somewhere on the farm, he had never seen them before. This was definitely not from around here.

Raliv reached into the crevice of the chair seat and pulled out a very small piece of paper. There was barely any room to write anything at all. The writing was tiny and Raliv had to hold it at arm's length away from his eyes to try to focus:

So much string! Thanks. You have more privacy than you want. People care. Let them.

Raliv felt a little bad for telling Pan to respect his privacy. Whoever this was, they were right. Raliv did have far more privacy than he wanted, and certainly more than was healthy. Family was constantly asking what he needed, and he had come to the farmhouse from the cabin one afternoon to find a casserole Mrs. Phelps up the road had left for him, along with a note offering condolences and assuring him she was someone he could rely on. He had thoroughly enjoyed the casserole, but he had yet to reply to Mrs. Phelps, and he had delayed having family come because he didn't want to be a burden. So instead, he had retreated into an unadorned life of chores and alternating between the cabin and the farmhouse.

He looked at the geode still in his hand. Colleen would have loved the raw beauty of it. Raliv loved it. He put the stone into his pocket, next to the flute. He took the pad and pen out of his other pocket and started writing:

The crystals are amazing. Thank you. Did you find this on the farm here? If so, where? I've given you a name, by the way. Pan. Being a woodland person who gave me a flute. I'm sorry if I was rude. I am okay with your being here. Please take good care of all that is on the land. Is there anything you need?

And then, he signed it.

Raliv

Raliv tore off the note from the pad, folded up the paper and wedged it into the chainsaw mark in the seat, and put the pad in his pocket. Then had to chuckle at his own lack of attention. Taking the pad and the pen out of his pocket, he put them on the chair for Pan. He returned to the truck.

At the cabin, Raliv filled the water heater attached to the woodstove, swept the floor, and then went out to the woodpile, still substantial from the remainder of the tree they had had to take down, and split logs for the stove and the fireplace. His back caught him up on one swing and then maintained an ache as he kept swinging the axe into the thick, white wood.

He decided to power through the discomfort. It was only a muscle ache caused by lack of use, and that meant he needed to do even more, rebuild his strength. It was how he had always dealt with such minor maladies in the past. He continued splitting wood for several minutes until he decided the pile was satisfactory and his back was probably loosened enough. He left the axe wedged into the tree trunk he used for his splitting base. Then he went to the little shed behind the cabin where he kept a few tools and took out the leaf rake to clear out where the leaves had blown down the hillside and onto the little flower garden.

By the time he had finished, the afternoon was waning. It had grown cooler. When he looked up, the clouds had blown away. He decided to stay at the cabin again that night. He had cleaned the litter box that morning, and Felicity had food and water, so she would be fine. Raliv went inside, started a fire in the cookstove, and put on the tea kettle. His back hurt. He leaned up against the counter and ate a can of Vienna sausages and then a small can of peaches. He made his orange pekoe tea and went back outside to sit at the picnic table.

As it grew dusky, the tree frogs down at the beaver pond started their creak-creaking, first one, then ten, then quiet for a moment, then thirty. It was a concert of the evening, as he and Colleen had called it. A cardinal sent out a "toowee-toowee-toowee-wee-wee-wee."

A squirrel jumped from one branch end to another, pausing while the receiving branch bobbed precariously. The squirrel scurried up the branch, then froze, head outstretched, observing. Raliv watched the squirrel pause on the fork of a heavier bough and then sit on its haunches and twirl a nut from last fall in its tiny hand-like claws, gnaw a bit, twirl, gnaw. The sky eventually grew deep purple with gentle stripes of red and pink. Now the chorus of tree frogs was loud and nonstop.

Raliv sat in the growing darkness and cold, thinking about all the times he and Colleen had spent sitting at this very table, dreaming, planning, and just enjoying the abundance of life around them. She had been everything he once held to be true, her and their love, and now that was gone. She was gone. What could now be true? Could he accept anything at all to be true if it could then be taken away? Surely, if truth was transient, then it wasn't true, by definition.

But he did still have the love, the love he had for Colleen. That love remained even though Colleen was gone. Would that love somehow live beyond even him? He wanted to think so but couldn't find a place to put that idea. Maybe he could just love her and not try to name it. Perhaps the less we know, the more we name, just like Pan had said. And maybe love isn't truth, only our expression of it. And the truth is something more, something deeper within us, something we only take out and see when our hearts are broken.

A pewee landed on the table and eyed Raliv curiously. Raliv wanted to capture the moment of this little simple bird, no doubt living in one of the nooks and crannies of the exterior of the cabin, sitting there looking at him, just as he was having these heavy thoughts come to him. It was such a backdrop of his life: the weight of the loss in sharp contrast to all of life going on around him, unmoved and unbowed.

Then he remembered he had the cell phone with its camera.

He slid his hand into his jacket pocket, slowly raised the phone up, and slid the camera app open. He snapped a picture from his hip just as the bird flitted off. He checked the picture. There was the bird, looking ready to fly off just as he had taken the picture. Raliv was glad he had captured the moment.

He started feeling chilly, even with his jacket zipped up tight, so he stood to go inside and a muscle caught up and sent a sharp pain down his back. He retreated stiffly into the cabin. It was still warm from his making the tea, and he welcomed the relief from the chill. When was it supposed to get cold? He tried to remember.

He was still holding the phone and looked at the picture again. The little bird was still there, ready to flee. He lit the oil lamp and sat down at the desk. He pulled out a piece of paper and a pencil and tried to draw the shape of the bird, its potential for flight so evident. Using the photo as his guide, he outlined the pewee, then began shading in the colorations. Since it was a black and grey and white bird, the pencil worked fine to give the drawing some depth, a bit of roundness.

Raliv worked for a long time on the drawing. His back was complaining more insistently so he finally decided he would just lie down for a minute and let his back relax some. That was all he really needed, a quick rest, then he could get up and maybe build a fire in the fireplace, have a small glass of bourbon, play his recorder.

Where was that recorder? Raliv turned to locate it with his eyes and his back twinged hard. Raliv stood with some difficulty. Okay, just a rest. He retrieved the geode from the jacket pocket and placed it on the windowsill above the bed so the morning light could shine through it. He put the phone on the little nightstand by the bed, then lay across the white comforter to let the muscle in his back relax. He pulled the pale blue blanket from the footboard over his arms and tried to let the muscle calm itself.

Chapter 6
The Visitor

The visitor awoke early. The rain had stopped in the night, and he wanted to retrieve the gift he had planned for Raliv early, before the day got late. He had seen the greens growing near the creek bed. He worried that the rains might have raised the water level, but they were still there. He picked them and washed them in the running stream and shook the water off as best he could and put them in the plastic bag.

He wanted to go early to the big chair and leave his gift and a note to say thank you. The sardines were such a treat for a man who had no seasonings except what he could find in the wild. He had eaten one can and even drank down the oils at the bottom, enjoying every bit of the almost exotic flavor from his usual diet. He rinsed out the can and scrubbed it with sand from the creek bed. He also saved the pull-off top.

He never knew when either one might come in handy. Perhaps the can was another pan for him to use if he wanted to heat something quickly. Maybe it could be a drinking vessel. The top was shiny. If he wanted a mirror, he might polish it up, although he doubted he ever wanted to use a mirror again. But he didn't have to decide just now. It would present itself in due time.

He stored the cleaned tin and top along with the unopened

can in his rucksack, then ate a small handful of arugula he had saved for himself and pulled out the ever-shrinking envelope to write his note. He figured he would need to walk up to the highway and find some other piece of paper soon. He obviously wouldn't use the letter he still could not bring himself to look at again. He might someday, but not yet. He wanted to write more, but there simply wasn't enough paper. He wanted to say thank you, but he also wanted to say he was never a threat to the land. It simply was not in him.

This was his path, the one he had chosen. He himself had felt grief and had had to come to the conclusion, as he supposed all people do, that his time would come. It was a deliberate choice to find a way that he could walk again. He would laugh again and live again. It would be his renaissance. He had had to finally decide that it could only be true if he made up his mind for it to be so. He could not be passive, waiting for his sorrow to pass, waiting to feel better. He had to grab life and to push forward.

Life is brief and fleeting, he knew. Waiting to heal was a path to death. And so he had undertaken this lifestyle, living off the land and moving, walking on. This is what worked for the visitor, and he could no more harm the land he held in such reverence than he could remove a leg and continue to walk.

He wanted to say all that, but there was no room. Instead, he wrote the simple note and carried it with the greens along the narrow trail through the woods up to the big chair. As he made his way, he listened for the truck. He hadn't heard it yet, but that did not mean he could not be surprised. But he liked that Raliv drove the noisy truck. It gave the visitor plenty of warning.

The temperature was warmer than the cold rain and that too felt good. As he stepped into the field to approach the chair, a rabbit darted along the edge of the tree line then into the grass. The visitor made a note to put a snare up in the area. Daffodils had enjoyed the rain, pushing open their yellow heads. A frog leaped from the edge of the pond into the water with a splash.

He left the greens and his note and looked up at the sky. It was maybe going to be better weather now. Then he heard the truck revving and grinding along the muddy road, so he quickly retreated into the trees and stood motionless. Raliv stepped out of his truck and came and sat on the chair. He opened the bag and sniffed it and gave up a smile. The visitor liked that. Then he wrote a note while he sat there, using a pad of paper and a pen that glinted light from a brightening sky. When the old man left and the visitor heard the rumble of the truck move up towards the farmhouse, he stepped over to the big chair.

On the seat of the chair was an entire ball of white string. The visitor had to smile to himself at that gift. What a surprise. He glanced up at where the rabbit had been. He could keep his shoes laced and trap rabbits now. There were so many things he could do with string, and here was an entire ball of it. This surely meant that Raliv was okay with his being there, but then he read the note.

The old man wasn't convinced yet. He was still challenging why the visitor felt he had any right to be there, and now was asking for privacy. He had mentioned Colleen. That must be who Raliv was grieving for. The visitor looked towards the farmhouse. That old man had just as much privacy as the visitor had in his life, in his own way. If the visitor had cut off people from his life, so had Raliv. But the visitor had noticed cars driving up and folks go to the door and even go inside. People cared about Raliv in a way they maybe didn't care about the visitor, or maybe he hadn't let them. He wondered if they cared even now, so many years later. What if they cared and simply could not find him? He tried to shake off the feeling by returning to the present in his hand.

The string felt like such an extravagance. If the visitor had learned that enough was plenty, here was an embarrassment of riches. What could he give Raliv in return? He walked the short distance to the trees, then cut an angle down the hillside, stopping to pull over a sapling and set a snare near where he had seen the rabbit before and arranging a few fallen branches to steer the prey into the trap. So much string to work with.

Back at his camp, the visitor finished tanning the rabbit pelt and stretched it on a circle of wood he had made by bending a long green twig from one of the cottonwood trees he had found near a beaver pond. It was supple wood, yet strong enough to hold its shape. Then he had an idea. He ate a quick bite of salted venison, then strode along the creek to the beaver pond and took another twig, smaller than the other one. He took it back to his camp and started tying knots around the stick he had bent into another circle.

He tied knot after knot. He had learned how to do this from a woman he once knew who sometimes traveled with him when he was younger, but she finally grew weary of the road. She said goodbye and drifted away from him. It was painstaking work, tying the knots and keeping it as even as possible, but it wasn't as if the visitor had other responsibilities to attend to.

Thinking about the woman reminded him of the crystal she had once given him. She had picked up the small round stone from a dry stream bed out west and they had cracked it open and found it full of beautiful purple quartz. He would share that with Raliv. The woman had given him the stone when she left and said she hoped it would bring some light into his life. He would give it to the old man now to bring light into his life. It had made the visitor happy to look at it for a while after she had left, but then it somehow became a memory of something else lost.

Then, alone, he had come to mourn her leaving, had decided he could avoid being hurt by avoiding people altogether. The woman would likely be sad to know it was a hurtful memory now. He would pass it along to Raliv, for whom it could bring some happiness, he hoped, or at least some brightness. He wondered just where the woman might be now. She was a good person, he recalled. Just now, he liked the memory.

He stopped knotting the string and rummaged again through his bag. He found the feathers he had picked up at the end of last summer. He took those out and put them close to the string. He found the geode and held it up to the light. It really was quite lovely. He was happy to share it with Raliv. He wanted to help Raliv feel better. He had asked for privacy, but that wasn't what the old man needed, the visitor knew. He needed support and family close by. It was what the visitor had given up when he took to the wilderness. Surely the old man could not retreat in the same way.

Retreat.

Is that what he had done? Had he simply retreated from the world after getting the letter? There was the letter right there in the sack where he had pulled the stone. He blinked. A breeze stirred the leaves behind him, shaking him from his reverie. He pushed the bag closed and shoved it back into the little shelter. The little stream trickled along, heading forever downhill. The visitor planned to follow it to its source, uphill, and eventually go as high as he could in the mountains. No one cared if he headed to the mountains, and no one would look for him there.

A squirrel barked at him from a black gum tree. Tiny pink buds were pushing out on the poplar trees. The little dented pot of bone broth was boiling softly. The fire was very low now and he decide to go check his trap. He could be there and back in short order. And he needed to stop remembering, at least for now.

He walked quickly, quietly, along the deer trail to where he had placed the snare. The day was warming, and he felt both energized by that and yet tired from the need for more food. He didn't want to eat the other can of sardines yet, but all the rain had made trapping much harder, and cooking impossible. He hoped he had a rabbit. He might eat the whole thing, if it wasn't too big.

When he reached the spot where he had set the snare, he found that he had not caught a rabbit but had trapped a woodcock instead. He loved woodcock. It wasn't as much meat as a rabbit, but he savored the flavor. This was a good day.

The visitor felt satisfied after eating his roasted bird. He couldn't remember the last time he had had both fish and fowl in the same week. He sat that night next to his small campfire, warming a stone and gazing into the flames. Tying knots in the string until it grew too dark to see clearly, he then played softly on his recorder he had finished making. He still wanted to decorate it, but there was time for that. He slept well with a full stomach, a warmed stone next to him in the hut.

He was up early the next day, feeling refreshed from the sleep and excited to be sharing the crystal with the old man. He was at the big chair just after dawn, his feet wet from a heavy dew that had fallen. He was eager to leave the stone and the short note that he hoped would help relieve some of Raliv's pain by getting him to reach out to his friends and his family.

The meadow was just waking up as he took long steps through the forest then across to the chair. He was careful to take a different route each day so as not to leave a trail. An eastern meadowlark sat on a scrappy juniper top, singing its flute-y song. Wild turkey hens made purring, waking-up sounds in tall ash trees nearby in the woods. A small red fox trotted along the edge of the field, stopped long enough to look back at the visitor, then hopped into the tree line. A breeze began stirring.

He left the note and the geode on the chair, then slipped over to the other side of the pasture to set another snare and to wait for Raliv to come by. He hoped the old man was as excited about the present as he himself had been with the string. And he hoped Raliv felt better today.

The rumble of the old truck told the visitor Raliv was heading toward him. The visitor had long ago learned to distinguish the sounds of vehicles approaching or leaving, changing in pitch like a train whistle going past. He stood in a stand of poplar trees and watched.

The old man was out early as well. He watched Raliv pick his way across the field and pick up the stone. The visitor had to smile when Raliv's eyes lit up. He was glad he had shared it. Then Raliv scribbled a note, paused, put the pad down, and walked back to his truck. When the growling truck motor had faded away over the ridge, the visitor stepped back out and went to the chair.

It was perfect: a pad of paper to continue the communication. Maybe he was helping Raliv. He hoped so. Then he read the note. He let out an involuntary laugh at being named "Pan." That was a new one. He realized that to Raliv, he just might be otherworldly. Then he read the part about being welcome. That was the real gift. That made him happier than he had felt in a long time. Raliv had asked him what he needed, then given him exactly what he needed.

From the corner of his vision, he saw the sapling he had set the snare on whip upright. At the end of the string, a quail flapped. The visitor, now Pan, felt his eyes widen. Yes, this was turning into a very good place to be.

Chapter 7
Raliv

When Raliv awoke the next day, he had the brief sensation of not knowing exactly where he was. It was an odd feeling. It wasn't that he didn't know whether he was at the cabin or at the farmhouse: he truly didn't know where he was for just a moment. It was as if he might be anywhere in the world, just not someplace he knew.

It was both a little frightening and a little liberating. But then he blinked and focused and knew he was sideways across the bed in the cabin, still lying flat on his back. Had he even moved? He tried to sit up and realized he had probably not moved or that pain in his back would have awakened him.

He gathered himself up with some difficulty, pushing himself sideways with his arm until he was in a seated position. He still had his clothes on, a tattered pair of khakis he had once worn to teach classes in that served as farm pants now, and a button-up denim shirt. Sitting on the edge of the bed, he dug a knuckle into his back. He leaned forward and gained his feet onto the rag rug with the help of gravity and walked stiffly across the room towards the kitchen area.

His back had tightened up in the night so much, he could barely walk. He leaned over to pick up a few pieces of the split wood he had brought in the night before to start the fire for coffee, but the pulled muscle reminded him quickly and harshly that it was not ready to make that move. Freezing in place, he then stood slowly, carefully. Rather, he stood up as much as his back would allow, which was not a lot.

"Crap." Raliv grimaced. He looked out the corner of his eye without turning his head, much less his body, at Colleen's chair at the drop leaf table. "I guess I overdid things yesterday, sweetheart. Ouch." He tried to decide if he wanted coffee enough to try bending over again and then realized he was bent over, of a sort. Perhaps it was more hunched over than bent, but it felt awkward.

He stepped carefully, stiffly, back across the room and sat gingerly at the kitchen table. "Well, this is bad." He glanced up at Colleen's chair. "I've wrenched it good this time." He was in such pain, he wondered if he could even make it out to the truck.

Maybe he should try to send a message to John on the cell phone. The signal was spotty even for a message, but he decided that might be the prudent thing to do. Raliv could barely move. He should send a message to John, and John would be glad to help. He was always asking to help out. He needed to let John help him, needed to let him care. And John would help him get back to the house. He could send a note to his son and then Raliv could hobble over and just sit in his big chair and play his recorder until John came and helped him.

John would likely want to take Raliv to the doctor, but Raliv figured he knew what his doctor would say. She was a straight-forward, blunt woman who always told him the truth, even when he didn't know if he wanted it. She would say, "You're getting older. Rest. Take ibuprofen. Give it a week." She might even swat his arm for trying to act like he was a youngster and splitting wood all alone on the back of his farm.

Raliv stood again, already learning a little which moves he could make and which he could not. He shuffled over to the little table to get the phone. He bent over slowly and picked it up to look at the screen. It was dead. He had planned to recharge it back at the house, but since he had never gone back, it was out of battery.

The sun through the window above the bed sent a pink light onto the comforter. The geode. He sat on the bed and put his hand on the pink light, as if he might feel the texture of it. On the back of his hand, the pinkness disappeared, so he moved his hand to let the ray return to the comforter. It looked like he was on his own.

Raliv made up his mind that he could make it through this on his own. He would have to, but carefully, gingerly. The twinge in his back was intense. Besides, if he drove himself, he could stop at the chair and get a message from Pan. And leave one.

He still hadn't told John or anybody else about this visitor and wasn't sure how it would go. He wanted to tell John about Pan. Actually, he wanted to tell anyone. But he also wanted to keep it a secret, and for this, he could offer no explanation. Was he hoarding a friendship? Was it even possible to do so?

Raliv eyed his boots across the room. Putting those on would involve some bending, but what choice did he have? His stomach growled and seemed to shake him from his thoughts. His meager dinner had left him hungry this morning. Was there anything at all to eat that didn't involve cooking? Raliv stood slowly. Perhaps it was loosening, or perhaps he was just figuring out how he could manage to move without twisting his back. He took a moment to steady himself, holding onto the edge of the desk.

He looked down at his support and saw the pencil sketch he had done of the pewee from last night. It wasn't half bad, he decided. He picked it up to look at it more closely, and the bending over to do so reminded him he was not done with the pulled muscle. He grimaced, then held the picture up to inspect it. He had crosshatched it well enough that the bird looked round and full.

His mother had taught him to draw. She herself had been an artist but was also quite flighty and had been in and out of his life since he was six. She had abandoned him and his siblings any number of times over the years, only to return later with imaginative and hardly believable tales about what had pulled her away, until her return was always a harbinger of her leaving and they had all learned the lesson well enough to not regard her return with any permanence. She finally passed away, penniless and alone in Kansas City, still trying to break into the art world with her allegorical, fanciful oil paintings. If she had been unreliable, at the least, she had taught Raliv to draw during one of the times she was present in his life.

He put the drawing down, dropping it the last few inches to keep from bending further, and shuffled to the pantry to see if there was anything at all that sounded like breakfast. Inside, he found a granola bar which made him far happier than a granola bar should make anyone, but at least he would not have to start a fire.

Raliv leaned back against the doorway to eat the bar where he stood. Taking the weight off his back provided some relief. He stood, leaning, munching away on the breakfast bar, and let his eyes adjust to the dark of the pantry further. There, propped up against the wall just to the right of the door, was one of Raliv's fishing poles, a light duty spinner rig. Above it on a shelf were the few pieces of tackle he kept here at the cabin, just enough to occasionally fish in the beaver pond.

He looked at it without much intent when he realized what Pan needed was some fishing tackle. It made perfect sense. Pan said he rarely got fish. And Raliv remembered that Pan probably knew where the bamboo patch was. He was so excited about his revelation, he almost forgot about his back as he reached for the spool of fishing line that was not far from used up but had plenty left for a cane pole.

His back tightened but he was too excited to let it stop him. He grabbed a few hooks and half a dozen split shot weights and cupped them in his hands as he turned and made his way slowly and stiffly to the kitchen area. In a drawer next to the sink stand, he pulled out a large plastic zip bag and dropped it all in, including the line.

His enthusiasm up from the prospect of taking his

brainstorm to Pan, Raliv felt a new energy, although the bending to put on his boots was every bit as unpleasant as he had feared it would be. He wrestled on his jacket, trying hard not to bend in any manner, and only then did he think to look out the window, curious as to what the weather might be.

The cabin was quite chilly, but the heavy logs it was made from meant it was usually chilly even in the heat of summer. Outside was sunny with a pale blue, cloudless sky. He felt his pocket. The flute was there. But he almost forgot to get another notebook of paper since he had left the other pad with Pan.

He sat carefully at the desk to rummage through it. He had paper everywhere. It was a legacy from his teaching days. He always had reams of paper stashed away. He found a pad and decided he might write this note ahead of time, since sitting on the chair might prove painful. Then he felt in his jacket pocket for the tiny piece of paper from yesterday's note. He wanted to be sure and answer Pan. He reread the short note, then picked up and clicked the ballpoint lying there, and began writing:

```
Yes, people do care, and not only
do I need to let them, I need to show
them I care about them. I not only need
to be loved, I need to be able to love.
Thank you for reminding me. Here is
some fishing gear. You know where the
cane is. If the ospreys haven't emptied
it, the pond rarely gets fished. It's
supposed to get very cold. Will you be
okay?

Raliv
```

Raliv put the note into his jacket pocket and labored towards the door. As he passed the kitchen counter, he picked up the bag of tackle. Without bending at all, he retrieved the phone from the bedside table as he went by and put it into his jacket pocket.

When he opened the cabin door, it was already much colder than he had realized. A brisk breeze was fluttering the budded-out leaves on the maple trees. The jacket he wore was not nearly heavy enough for this level of chill. No matter, he thought. I will be okay in the truck. But that cold snap was bearing down hard already.

He did not lock the door of the cabin this time. He walked, hunched over and stiff, to the truck, wondering how ancient he must look, a crotchety old man limping, scuffling across the woodland garden towards his rusty pickup. If this was what he had come to, Raliv wasn't at all sure he liked it. Climbing into the truck caused some discomfort, although getting out of the chilly wind felt immediately better on that count. The truck grumbled to life on the first try, which was a huge relief, and Raliv steered down the path towards the meadow. He tried the heat on the truck, but the motor was not warmed enough to give any help, so he turned it off.

In the pasture, the Johnson grass was bent over from the wind and it looked very cold out in the open. Raliv pulled up next to the garden area, still being mindful of the bulbs, although some of them would no doubt be nipped by this cold snap, He left the truck running so the engine could heat up, and climbed out. He landed on the ground with both feet, having twisted in the seat to let gravity help him out. Even landing with two feet twinged his back some.

He walked stiffly, bent over, towards the chair, so hunched over he actually had to look up to see in front of himself. He pushed the back of his hand into his back reflexively, although it made no difference in the pain. He hoped he wasn't too early to get a message from Pan today since he was unlikely to be able to return later.

He squinted in the morning sun to see the chair. There was something already there. He was glad for that. If he could have quickened his pace, he would have. As he neared the chair, he could see that it looked like another rock. If it was another geode, that would not be at all bad, thought Raliv. He could keep one at the cabin and one at the house. Weren't they supposed to bring good luck or something?

It was a rock, but only a small brown pebble, polished by creek water over decades into a smooth ovoid, but underneath it was a note and something with feathers on it. Raliv picked up the note to keep it from blowing away and held it in one hand, then picked up the present.

It was a dreamcatcher. Pan had taken the string Raliv had given him and used part of it to tie into an intricate webbing and all of it was encased in a circle of wood. Raliv inspected it more closely. At the top, where a small strip of tanned rabbit pelt made a hanger, he could see the wood beneath. It looked like a cottonwood twig, pulled into a neat circle through the webbing. The beaver pond was surrounded by cottonwoods that sent their fluffy seeds adrift each summer, piling up on the water and rocks around the pond. Where the string was attached, the twig was tightly wrapped in the rabbit leather. Dangling from the circle were two long strands of string, weighted down with crinoids, small fossilized cylindrical fragments with holes in them.

Carefully tied to one string was a blue jay feather. The other held a bright red cardinal feather. The circle itself was only a couple of inches across, and the trailing lines less than a foot, but the detailed work on it captured Raliv immediately. He held it up by the hanger, the quickening breeze pulling it sideways. It was beautiful. It was something he never would have thought of finding there. It was just what he needed, something to capture the dreams, sending the bad ones away, and allowing the good ones to filter down through the feathers into his head. It was exactly what he needed and wanted.

Then he looked back at the note, unfolding it with one hand so he would not need to put the gift back down on the chair. It was a longer note this time, and Raliv felt good about his gift of paper just then:

Pan. I love that name. I have gone

75

by many names, and been called by many others, but Pan may be my favorite. The crystal was a gift from a friend on my travels. I am glad you like it. You ask me what I need. I don't need much. I do not want you to be concerned. The forest gives me all I could ask for and that makes me richer than most. What is it you ask for?

Pan

Raliv read the note and looked up at the tree line. It was getting cooler by the minute. Who was this person who brought such wonderful gifts to him? Were they watching him even now? But Raliv didn't strain to see. If Pan wanted to not be seen, Raliv was okay with that. He was curious, absolutely, but he would defer to Pan's wishes.

Another stiff breeze brought Raliv back. He stood stiffly, needing to take a quick step sideways to get his balance. He put the note he had written and the fishing gear in the bag under the stone on the chair. Raliv shuffled back to the truck, carefully carrying the note and the dreamcatcher in one hand, and climbed back in. He lay the gift and the note on the seat next to him and admired the handiwork again for just a moment. This time when he twisted the knob on the heater, a steady stream of warm air blew out of the vents.

What would Raliv ask for, he wondered. What, in all of the trying times in attempting to make sense of his life now without Colleen, would he ask for? It was a very good question, he decided, one he would need to think about.

Back at the farmhouse, Raliv slid out of the truck onto both feet again. He tried to walk quickly to the door to get out of the chill in the air, but a kind of rapid shuffle was all he could manage. Felicity heard the key in the door and rushed into the kitchen to greet him. Raliv reached down to pet her but the ache in his back made him shorten the petting. He removed his boots by the back door and wended his way to the living room to plug in the phone at the port by Colleen's chair. It turned on when he got the cord attached and he pushed the button to call John's cell phone.

"Hello?" John's voice sounded like he was either busy with something else or worried.

Raliv sat in his chair gingerly, the cord draping across the little table. "Hi, John." He placed the dreamcatcher on the small table between the chairs, keeping the note in his pocket.

"Hi, Pop. Is everything okay?" It had been worry.

"Yeah, but I twisted my back and it's pretty sore." Sitting in the chair didn't hurt so much, so he wondered if he was exaggerating a bit. He leaned forward and realized he was not.

"Do you need to go to the hospital?" Raliv could hear John's voice go up in pitch.

"No. No. Really, I don't. But I need to rest up some, take it easy. I was wondering if you would bring me a sandwich or something, so I won't have to cook. It's hard to stand for long just now."

"Of course, Pop. I'll be over in twenty minutes."

"No, you don't have to drop everything. I'm fine. Just pulled a muscle. It can wait until tonight if you need to. But I wouldn't mind a sandwich from Jolene's, if you come that way."

"Okay." John's voice returned to normal. "What kind of sandwich would you like?"

"Well, . . ."

"Reuben. I know what you want. Jolene makes a good Reuben, doesn't she?"

"She does indeed." Raliv let himself recall the salty, hearty flavor. His mouth watered thinking about it.

"You got it, Pop." Then the phone went dead. Raliv had intended to ask when John might be over, if he was not in fact coming now, but it was too late, and he would not call him back just to ask that. It wasn't as if Raliv had someplace he needed to be. The truth was, he could wait until John got off from work, but the granola bar simply wasn't a whole lot of food and he was already feeling a bit hungry.

It was early yet, still before noon. But he had told John to wait and now, Raliv just needed to try to relax and let his back loosen up. He was still wearing his jacket, so he pulled out the recorder, sat back in his chair, and played through the two songs he knew. He played them again, and a third time.

Felicity came in, looked up at him, then jumped up onto the ottoman in front of him and immediately fell asleep. What was that song Colleen had enjoyed so much, a simple French folk song? He had bought her a tiny music box at a shop on rue Buci in Paris that played a bright but vaguely plaintive version of it when she turned the small crank. "Au Clair de la Lune," that was it. He remembered it now. Many evenings, as they prepared for bed, he had picked up the box and played the song, and it always brought a smile to her pretty face, a reminder of travels taken and travels still planned.

Raliv played the notes slowly. It was a simple song and he figured it out quickly. He had played it through a third time when he heard the backdoor open and close.

"Pop?" It was John. He had made it over in twenty minutes, or less, it seemed. Raliv let himself smile. He heard a clunk as something was placed on the kitchen table.

"In here, Son." Raliv considered rising to greet his son, but when his back sent a quick pang up his shoulder, he decided he was fine where he was. John came into the living room, his coat still on, and gave Raliv a sideways look. He had a large white paper sack in his right hand. Felicity sat upright, then bolted from the room.

"Was that you playing, Pop?" He sat in Colleen's chair and Raliv suppressed the urge to tell him not to. John opened the bag and pulled out two cardboard cups with plastic tops, put them on coasters on the little table, which was getting crowded, and then brought out two sandwiches wrapped in white shiny paper. Then he reached back in and lifted a paper boat filled with

French fries, which he handed over to Raliv's outstretched hand.

"Oh, fries. I love fries." Raliv slid the recorder on the table next to his drink while John handed over the food. Raliv balanced the food items on his lap.

"I know, Pop." John shot him a quick smile. He reached back into the bag and pulled out a handful of ketchup packets and, cradling them, handed them all over to Raliv.

"None for you?" Raliv cupped his hands to receive the packets.

"I like mustard on mine." John placed his food on the ottoman Felicity had just vacated, then stood and went into the kitchen. He came back with an unopened squeeze jar of brown mustard. He went about setting up his own lap full of food, but Raliv was already eating fries dipped generously into the ketchup he had pushed out of the tubes.

John paused long enough to appreciate how eagerly Raliv was digging in. He nodded, then opened the jar and squeezed a big dollop of mustard onto the side of his own paper boat of fries. "So," John pointed at the table with a French fry he had already bitten in half, "you're getting pretty good at that little flute, huh, Pop?"

"Well, it's a simple tune. It wasn't hard to figure out." Raliv took a big bite from the sandwich. The sauerkraut made his jaws tighten. The rich salty corned beef and the sweetness of the dressing all mingled together in his mouth, and just on the back of his tongue was the sharp, bitter swiss cheese. It was the best thing he had tasted in months, since before, when Colleen was not yet ill, from when things were okay.

John eyed him, as if trying to read his thoughts. Raliv put the sandwich down on the waxy paper it had come in. "My god, John, that may be the finest sandwich ever made." Raliv took a sip from his drink. Unsweetened tea. That boy knew his old man.

"Well," John chewed on a bite from his identical sandwich and gave him another smile, "my father always told me, 'Hunger makes the best sauce.'" This brought a smile to Raliv, too.

He had at first thought he would eat only half the sandwich and save the other half for dinner, but before he even thought about it again, the sandwich was gone and he was dragging the last few fries through the remnants of ketchup. John wadded up the paper from his own meal and tossed all of it back in the paper sack, then reached over and took Raliv's. As he stood to take it to the kitchen, he paused and looked down at the table. He cocked his head to one side, curious. "What's this?" He reached with his free hand and picked up the dreamcatcher.

"Oh, that. It's just a little gift someone gave me. It's a . . ."

"Dreamcatcher," John finished. "It's gorgeous." He held it up higher so the strands could dangle. Then he lowered it and looked at his father and grinned. "'A gift from someone.' What's going on with you?"

"Nothing." Raliv shrugged, lying.

"Okay. Okay. I guess you'll tell me what's going on when you're ready, Pop." He held the dreamcatcher up again to admire it then placed it gently back on the table. Raliv appreciated that he had been careful with it, although it didn't seem especially fragile, but it was his present, and Raliv valued that. John eyed his father curiously for just a moment, then went into the kitchen and threw away the trash. He walked back into the living room, rubbing his hands together. "I got you some soups that are ready to eat. You can just put them into the microwave tonight for your supper."

"I can't imagine I will ever be hungry again." Raliv patted his stomach.

"Well, I hope you are, Pop. It made me feel much better to see you enjoying your lunch." He turned towards the door. "I have to get back to the office. I have an important meeting this afternoon. Please have some of the soup tonight. You've been looking a bit haggard."

"Yeah, well, truth be told, I've been feeling a bit haggard." Raliv tried to stand to walk John out but his back caught him up. "Do me a favor before you go and get me the ibuprofen from the cabinet above the sink in the bathroom? It's on the second shelf, all the way to the left." John spun and walked down the hallway quickly. He was back in no time.

"Right there, where you said."

"Colleen's doing. She loved knowing where things were." Raliv allowed a soft memory to waft into his head. Colleen enjoyed having things organized. Her particular achievement was the pantry. She knew where everything in it was located. He would sometimes ask just to quiz her. "Honey, where's the sugar?" And she would answer with a smirk, knowing it was a test, "All the way to the left in the back about belly high." And that was exactly where it was.

"Dad," John handed over the bottle of pills, "Tina is making her amazing lasagna tonight. I thought the kids and I could come over tomorrow afternoon, visit a bit, enjoy some lasagna, maybe have a glass of wine."

"Kids are a bit young for wine, John." Raliv opened the ibuprofen bottle and took two with his tea, which was already getting a little watery. He wished they wouldn't put so much ice in the drinks.

"Ha." John was in the doorway now. "JJ has an indoor little league practice tomorrow at the gym at his school. We'll drop by after that, okay?"

"They start little league already?" Raliv shook his head. "When do they start two-a-days?"

John stood in the doorway, half turned towards the door. He smiled. "See you tomorrow, Pop. Kids'll be happy to see Grandad." Then he left.

After John left, Raliv tried to decide what he might do for the rest of the day. He glanced over at the little table and considered playing the recorder some, but he didn't really feel like it just now. He wanted to hang up the dreamcatcher above the bed, but he knew that was a bad idea with his back hurting. He hadn't watched television during the day in so long, he wondered if anything were on but the soap operas his grandmother used to watch. It was what he associated with daytime television. It didn't matter. He just didn't seem to be interested.

He was sitting there in his chair, waiting for the ibuprofen to start working, and trying to decide just what his back might allow him to do, when he remembered the note he had gotten from Pan, and the question Pan had left with Raliv: "What is it you ask for?"

Raliv pulled the note from his jacket pocket. He considered taking the jacket off now since he really didn't need it indoors, but it felt warm and comfortable so why remove it? He unfolded it and reread the note, just to be sure he remembered correctly.

What would he ask for? He sat back in his chair to consider it. He would ask for Colleen to be well, sitting next to him, and for them to be happy for a long time together. But that wasn't really what Pan was asking. It wasn't a question about changing the past, but about what Raliv might need or want now to navigate this grief, to find his footing again in this world he had been relegated to.

His memory returned to drawing the pewee the night before, and then to the drawing lessons when he was young. In some ways, where he stood should perhaps be familiar ground. Every woman he had ever loved and needed love from had left him. Why was he always the one still there, left behind, still standing there, trying to figure: was it him? Was it his fault? It must be.

Just that moment, he felt abandoned and unworthy of being loved, as evidenced by the fact he was alone. When he looked at himself, at the man inside beyond the surface, all he could see was a very all-alone man. Raliv wondered if that was indeed his destiny. A loner, a quirky old man hiding out in a hunting cabin, removed from everyone else so he might not be left again.

If he would just stay by himself, as lonely as that prospect was, he could never be abandoned again. But he knew he wasn't really alone. There were the boys, the grandchildren, and even Mr. and Mrs. Phelps down the road cared what happened to him. There were plenty of people who cared and who wanted to help. And, losing Colleen, no one was to blame. It just happened.

It was as if life figured out what he needed most by the choices he made, then, because life is heartless, it took it away, just to remind him his choices were of no consequence to the world writ large.

Raliv leaned forward. The pills were starting to work. He could still feel that his muscle was pulled, but it hurt less. He stood now and walked in small steps to the kitchen, removing his jacket. What would he ask for?

He hung his jacket on the coat peg by the back door and glanced around the kitchen. One hard part was by not going anywhere there was only this home he and Colleen had built, this world they had built, surrounding him to always keep him thinking about the life they would be living right now, the life they should be living right now. Together. It made it all so immediate and close and inescapable, and there was no one to tell that to, no one who could possibly understand.

Raliv gazed out the window towards the barn. Then, Raliv knew how to answer Pan's question.

Chapter 8

Raliv woke up early, having made an early evening of the night before. He had tied the dreamcatcher to a post on the bed then played his recorder sitting on the edge of the bed. He put the instrument in the bedside table, away from prying eyes. He wasn't ready yet to tell anyone about Pan.

Returning to the living room, he read the book he had started the week before, a novel about three old friends meeting up on a northeastern island, delving back into their friendship from their youth and a mystery about the girl they all loved. While the circumstances were completely different, reading about these old friends gathering made Raliv miss his own friends, some of whom he had known since childhood.

After reading for a bit, he had switched on the news in time for the energetic woman forecasting the weather to tell him that the next day, today now, would see the coldest temperatures of the current cold spell and up to three inches of snow was expected in the evening. Raliv knew he had to get out and warn Pan before John and the kids arrived.

It was, perhaps, foolhardy for Raliv to get out, but he was only going to go by the message chair and then make a quick run by the cabin to be sure everything was in order there. He shuffled into the kitchen in his bathrobe and slippers. There was still time to have some coffee. His back was still pretty tender. Scooping of the litterbox reminding him of that, but he had to admit, it felt somewhat better. Slowing himself down and taking the pills were helping.

Just before he had awakened, he had dreamed that he and Colleen were in a helicopter, heading to Pennsylvania to look at some land they were interested in, although in real life, they had never entertained living in Pennsylvania, in particular. In the dream, Colleen was flying the helicopter and was very adept at it, swooping around power lines and trees as if she had flown helicopters all her life. In the dream, Raliv had marveled at her skills and told her so, and she had accepted the compliment graciously.

It was a good dream. Raliv always liked it when Colleen came to him in dreams. When she did, it was always just in the normal course of whatever was happening in the dream, as if nothing had changed. But this one was different. It had seemed so lifelike, exhilarating, close. The images of the dream were still with him as he made his way across the kitchen.

He started to put on the regular coffee but opted to go for the espresso again. There was time for that. He ground the beans, packed them in the metal filter, poured water into the reservoir, and let it start its process. In the meantime, he fished out a frozen waffle and a single sausage patty from the freezer. The sausage patty clunked into the skillet. The toaster oven gave a warm glow on the frosty pastry.

When was the last time he had eaten a waffle? He actually only kept them around for the grandchildren and had forgotten he had this box until he went digging through earlier in the week before going to the grocery, checking to see what he might need. He couldn't recall when he might have bought them. Perhaps Colleen had, but they looked fine when he inspected them.

When it was all ready, he sat at the table, poured maple syrup over the waffle, and started eating. The sausage was tasty and satisfying, salty and a little spicy. The waffle tasted like cardboard with syrup on it. How did the kids eat it? Syrup cured a lot of evils, evidently. But the coffee was excellent, and its intensity gave him a caffeine boost almost immediately.

Pan and the Message Chair

The dishes rinsed and loaded in the dishwasher, Raliv returned to the bedroom and dressed, putting on his fleece-lined blue jeans that were such a godsend in cold weather and a heavy woolen shirt over a long-sleeved tee.

He checked Felicity's water and feeder, then headed for the front closet to pull out his heavy blue parka with the bright orange liner. He had had this coat since he was in college. It was stained and tattered on the edges, but was still the warmest, most reliable coat he owned, although Colleen was forever buying him new coats and sweaters, worrying about both his being warm and his looking like a vagabond. He put on the coat, his back complaining some, then returned to the bedroom for the extra set of sheets for the double bed at the cabin.

He spied the cellphone charging beside the bed and picked it up and shoved it into one of the many pockets on the parka. He had promised to carry it. After taking two more ibuprofen, he returned to the kitchen. He took a piece of paper and a pen from the desk and sat at the table to write his note to leave at the chair:

Good morning, Pan. I hope you are okay. Today is supposed to get very cold and a pretty heavy snow is forecast. I want you to stay in the cabin tonight. There is plenty of firewood and there are provisions in the pantry. Please make yourself at home there. It would be dangerous for you to stay outdoors tonight.

Thank you for the dreamcatcher. It is incredibly beautiful and is already working. Something to keep me from having bad dreams.

I have thought a lot about the question you asked me: what would I ask for? I would ask for a friend.

Raliv

The air outside was already cold when Raliv stepped out through the kitchen door. He could see his breath in the cold air. He pulled the wrinkled leather gloves out of his pocket and pulled them on his hands, balancing the sheets from one arm to the other. The gloves had been wet often enough that they were a bit stiff, but he finally wrestled them on, climbed into the truck, and placed the sheets on the bench seat next to him.

The motor had to be cranked a couple of tries, but then the old truck grumbled to life. A new battery was soon to be in the truck's future, he knew. The ground was already frozen, and the truck bounced along tire ruts made rigid by the cold. In the meadow, he glanced over to the chair, but it was empty still. The grass looked brittle, ready to break at the slightest touch.

Raliv decided to head to the cabin first. The puddles along the path where it wended through the woods were ice now. The flowers in Colleen's garden were going to be nipped as they so often were, coaxed out by the few days of promising weather only to be frozen by an unyielding cold snap.

At the cabin, Raliv thought about starting a fire in the cookstove, so the house would be warm for Pan. But he decided it would be dangerous to leave an unattended fire, so he worked in the cold, although inside the cabin was better than in the now windy, bone-chilling cold of the outdoors.

He changed the sheets, balling up the old ones and placing them outside on the picnic table. He swept the wood floor and spent several minutes sweeping hard on the rag rug. The sweeping reminded him to be careful of his back. He fluffed up the throw pillows on his and Colleen's chairs. The pile of wood inside the door was not huge but should be plenty for the night and Raliv had no interest in swinging the axe in the cold, or at all, just now.

As he was looking around the cabin to ensure it looked inviting, he saw the drawing he had done and picked it up again. He put it in his pocket to show John later. Raliv decided it was maybe the best drawing he had ever done.

He put away the broom and dustpan and headed for the door, but he stopped long enough to look at the photo on the mantle from the beach. What would Colleen think of Pan? She would approve of Raliv's generosity. He was certain of that. She was forever going out of her way to help others, even when Raliv had wondered if the man begging for change at the interchange of the highway wasn't just some guy taking advantage of the goodwill of kind-hearted people like Colleen. She didn't care, she had told him. It wasn't about what he did with the money. It was about her intentions when she gave him the money. It was a point he had no rebuttal for.

Raliv grabbed the sheets from the picnic table and hurried out to the truck. It was too cold to spend much time recalling a conversation. The sky was grey and heavy and the trees leaning over in the wind seemed to shiver. Having been driven earlier, the truck started up immediately. The engine was warm enough for the heater to begin working, and Raliv was relieved for the warmth.

He wondered again about leaving a fire going, but what if Pan didn't stay there? The place could burn down, although he had never had an issue with either the fireplace or the cookstove, so why either would choose to be a problem when he wasn't there made no sense. In a way, wouldn't it be better if either was going to stop up and maybe catch the creosote in the chimney afire for it to happen when no one was there? But no matter now. He had left a big box of wooden matches on the mantle. Pan would know how to start a fire.

Raliv bounced along in the truck towards the chair. He didn't have a gift for Pan but decided letting them stay in the cabin was probably present enough. How much did a woodland traveler need? If Raliv gave them a cast iron skillet, it would be too much. It would only weigh them down. No, Raliv needed to think about what made sense as a gift. Staying in the cabin was a good present.

Raliv tried to imagine Pan in the cabin but having no idea of their appearance made it hard. He did not worry that the place would be in any danger from his guest. Someone who could carve a recorder from bamboo or make a dreamcatcher from simple cotton twine was not someone who would ramshackle a cabin, if they even took him up on it, which he was not all certain they would.

Raliv pulled up to the chair, still mindful of the bulbs he and Colleen had planted, although the cold might have already made short work of them. Before he got out of the truck, he checked to see if he still had his note, then hurried as best he could with his back stiffening in the cold over to the chair.

He had seen through the windshield there was something there. On the chair was the plastic baggy he had put the fishing gear in. He picked up the bag by its zipper top, shoved his note into the crevice of the log, and hurried back to the truck that he had left running with the heat on.

Once in the truck, Raliv held up the bag. In it was a clay pinch pot bowl, small and roughly formed. Raliv opened the bag to take the little bowl out and was met by a strong scent of lavender, arnica, and peppermint. Raliv pulled his nose back but it wasn't an unpleasant odor, only a strong one. He sniffed the bag again and peered in.

The little bowl was filled with a liquid which was all but frozen in the cold, although the scent was clear enough. Also in the baggy was a note, which Raliv fished out now, still cradling the little bowl in his gloved left hand.

        Dear Raliv,

        This is a liniment I use when my
        back is hurting. It will help. Don't
        use a lot and be aware it might stain

things. Thanks for the fishing gear. I have already enjoyed a couple of little bluegill from the pond here. They are small but plentiful.

You are loved. Your family loves you. Friends and neighbors love you. If they are quiet now, it is because they don't know what you need, what you want. Tell them. And they want your love. You will always be able to love. More importantly, you will always have the love you shared with your wife. That never dies. Don't be afraid to hold onto it. Carry it with you proudly. You earned it.

Pan

Raliv looked out the windshield towards the opening of the ruined fence and the catalpa tree, which waved its heavy branches in the wind. He reread the note, letting it soak in. Then he looked at the little bowl again. Liniment was a great idea. He gently placed the baggy and the note on the seat next to him and drove back to the farmhouse.

By the time Raliv had taken off his extra clothes, applied a thin layer of the oily liniment, and put on his most tattered tee shirt, John and the grandchildren came busting in the door. The weather was as uninviting as it could be to staying outside. The ointment was already warming Raliv's back. He pulled on a sweatshirt and walked from the bedroom and found the three of them still in the kitchen, shivering.

"Come in. Come in." Raliv walked towards the children, arms outstretched. They dropped their coats onto the floor from their arms in a fluid motion, then ran over to Raliv, who had leaned forward now, and hugged him, one on each side. Felicity was likely hiding under the bed. She was always shy at first with visitors.

John stood there holding a long, flat baking dish in one hand and a brown paper sack that obviously had a bottle in it. He glanced at the coats on the floor and looked like he was ready to remind the children to hang up their coats but decided not to. Instead, he turned and placed the items he was holding on the kitchen table and hung the children's coats up on the row of pegs that served as a coat rack by the back door. Then he took his own off and hung it on the back of one of the cane-bottom chairs.

"Can we play with Dad's old toys, Grandad?" JJ was already making a beeline to the hall closet.

"Sure!" Raliv watched the two run off.

"You might want to visit with Grandad a moment?" John was saying, but Raliv held up his hand. Becky raced after her brother.

"It's fine, John. This is exactly what I want. The sound of them playing and being happy is just exactly what I need in a visit." John nodded his head and smiled. Then he came over and gave his father a long hug also.

"What's that smell, Pop?" He pulled back, a puzzled look on his face.

"Oh, just a bit of medicine for my back." Raliv reached back as if to remind himself. It was surprising how well the liniment was working.

"Huh. Smells very . . . herbal-ly. Nice." John turned now and took the baking dish off the table and slid it into the oven with the foil still on it. He pushed the buttons on the stove familiarly. The oven beeped and he turned back around. "Might take a while. It was in the car and it's really getting cold out there." He stiffened his arms and gave a shiver, both a demonstration of the cold and a recollection.

"Want some coffee, Son?"

"Yeah, I would. Might warm me up a little." He shivered again.

Raliv started the coffee, and while it brewed, he and John followed the sounds of the children playing into the living room. JJ had emptied the bin of Legos onto the wooden floor and was focused on whatever his imagination saw the few pieces he had pushed together becoming. Becky had taken out the old Matchbox cars that at one time had been Raliv's, before being passed down to his sons, and was lining them up in a parade.

"We're coming over to your house, JJ." Becky moved the lead car a foot, then the second, then the third.

JJ lowered his construction project and watched for a second, then reached down into the stack of plastic pieces and started pushing together larger flat pieces. "This will be my house." He focused on his project.

"Make me a house too, JJ." Becky hopped up.

Raliv stepped past them into his chair. John sat in Colleen's chair. They were both watching the kids. The children began to speak more softly, as if the make-believe world they were engaged in was no place for grown-ups.

"They play well together, John." Raliv nodded.

"Yeah, well, until they don't." He kept his gaze on the children.

"You and Brian were exactly the same way." Raliv too was staring at the children at play. The coffee maker beeped and Raliv started to get up, but John stood quickly and put his hand in a stop motion.

"I got it, Pop. Black?" John glanced down at his father.

"Yes. Thank you." Raliv usually only drank a single cup in the morning. His coffee was so strong, he only required that much to get him going. He hoped another cup wouldn't keep him awake.

When John returned with the two cups, the two of them sat together, watching the children play, talking about the things they generally talked about: sports, books, music. Every once in a while, one of the children would bring a toy over to either Raliv or John to explain what was going on in the ever-changing narrative of the game they were deep into, or to show what they had constructed from the plastic pieces.

Raliv would step on those pieces for at least a week after they left, although he really didn't mind. It was such a reassuring presence to have them here. They had been playing this way and talking for some time when the oven beeper sounded. Raliv looked down and his coffee cup was nearly empty.

How long had they been visiting and just being together? He realized as he stood that he had not felt this emotionally relaxed in a long while. Why didn't he feel this calm at the cabin, when there should be nothing there that might stress him? Or here at the farmhouse, either? John was already in the kitchen before Raliv managed to step past the two children playing, now each in their own reverie of pretend worlds.

"Lasagna's ready," John called from the kitchen.

"Daddy, we had lasagna last night." Becky let out a whine.

"Yeah," JJ added, but he didn't sound like he really objected, more like he was joining in on the protest, if half-heartedly.

"Would you kids rather have waffles?" Raliv leaned over them.

"Yeah! Waffles!" they cried in unison, jumping to their feet.

John stuck his head into the doorway. "Waffles? For lunch, Pop?"

Raliv shot him a grin. "Grandad's house." John smiled back at him and returned to the kitchen. Raliv came in to see the bubbling casserole half-filling the dish sitting on the stove top now, and his mouth immediately watered. He loved Tina's lasagna. "Besides, more for us," he said in a mock whisper.

John had thrown together a salad with what was left of the arugula and had add some chopped vegetables. Then John opened the bottle of wine and held it up for his father to see.

"Rioja okay?"

"Sounds wonderful." Raliv plated the waffles he had heated up in the toaster oven for his grandchildren and placed the bottle of syrup on a saucer between them on the table. JJ reached first and poured a generous coating of syrup on his plate. John turned and saw him do it too late to say anything, so he only sighed and shook his head.

Raliv nodded. Some things do not change.

Not to be outdone, Becky poured an even larger pool of syrup on her plate. John took the syrup and the saucer and placed them on the kitchen counter, out of immediate reach. The lasagna was as good as Raliv hoped. With the salad and the wine, he felt as spoiled as he could feel. After they ate, John made the kids wash their sticky hands in the bathroom while he himself cleaned up the kitchen. There was still a healthy square of pasta left for later that Raliv was already anticipating. He covered it up with foil and slid it into the refrigerator. He always considered lasagna a dish that improved with age.

When the four of them returned to the living room, John and Raliv took their wine glasses and the kids returned to the toys, but the worlds the children imagined now were necessarily different, since the time between before lunch and after lunch was a completely different epoch in the minds of children. Becky especially wanted to share what her "people" were doing in their cars now in the new game and where they were going, bringing them over to her Grandad's recliner and resting them almost tenderly on the arm of the chair. JJ became quiet, focusing intently on whatever construction he was undertaking. The Legos had been John's and he had enjoyed them for a long time as a child, even taking at least some of them on car vacation trips.

"Do you remember that first trip the four of us took together?" Raliv turned his head to address John but kept a focus on Becky as well, but then she was back down on the floor, playing with a different car. "Out west." He turned now to face his son better. "You took your Legos." Raliv nodded towards the pile on the floor.

"Of course. Jackson Hole. Tetons. Yellowstone." John took a sip of wine. "It was a great trip. Remember the horse ride? All the animals we saw? I really liked the big bull moose down in the shallows. He was impressive."

"Colleen always loved that area out west. She went there with her family several times."

"I always loved that she included us in everything. She was a great step-mother." John's gaze went unfocused for a moment and Raliv watched his son, watched him gathering another memory. "All those trips to the beach too. Man, she loved the beach."

"She really did. Funny thing is, she wasn't interested in going into the water much." Raliv took a sip of wine and set it down on the table. "She would wade a bit, but never in deep. It was more that she liked the waves and the sand and the sun. She would be so happy just sitting there next to the water, reading a book, for hours." Now Raliv stared off into space, into that familiar scene, so clear in his memory. Then he realized the room had grown quiet.

"Grandad?" Becky stood next to his chair now.

"Yes, sweetheart?" Raliv turned to face her, bringing himself out of the reverie.

"I miss Nana." She stared at him with large, blue eyes that looked on the verge of tearing up.

"Me too, honey." Raliv leaned over and hugged his granddaughter.

"Grandad?" This time it was JJ who had put down the toys and was kneeling next to his father.

"Yes, JJ?" Raliv turned to see JJ's face, so open and innocent and tender.

"Tell us some stories about you and Nana."

John started just a bit, as if this would be an intrusion or an unhappy task, but in truth, it was a welcome request. He wanted to talk about Colleen. He had been too reticent for too long. "I would be happy too." He gave his grandson a smile. Besides, it was exactly what Becky was asking for as well, if not as directly.

The children sat on the rug at John and Raliv's feet, and Raliv told them in a stream-of-consciousness storyline about Nana and Grandad, how they had met on a surprise blind date at a dive bar in their college town and how they had both known in short order that they were meant to be together. Then he told them about when Brian and John first met her and how genuine she had come across. And then there was the wedding, a slap-dash affair officiated by Raliv's friend who was a part-time chimney sweep, part-time farmer, and occasional preacher.

The children sat attentively, listening to the story of the first house they bought together, a split level in the suburbs, and about the times they traveled to various places around the country and overseas. John listened quietly, staring at the floor, occasionally sipping his wine. Eventually, JJ began working with the Lego pieces again, absent-mindedly pushing pieces together, and Becky started pushing the cars around. Raliv stopped and looked at the three of them and smiled.

"That's enough for now," he said. He took a drink from his wine glass as well.

John looked over at his father, his eyes brimming with tears, but he didn't let them fall. "Pop," his tone was one of appreciation. He looked at Raliv for a long moment. "We probably need to get going. Tina should be getting home from her meeting soon. She'll be wondering what got into us." Raliv nodded. Tina was involved in a variety of community groups, always helping out, and often volunteering when no one else seemed willing. John looked at the pile of toys as he stood. "Kids, pick up the toys now and put them back so you know where they are next time."

"Oh, I'll get those." Raliv also stood. His back was feeling better, but he was interested in another application of liniment, just to be sure.

"No, they can pick them up. Come on." He waved to his children and they quickly gathered the toys and put them back in the closet, much faster than if Raliv had had to bend over and pick them up. When John had herded them into the kitchen and pulled their coats on, the two men looked outside for the first time since they had eaten. Outside, they could not see the barn. The snow was coming down fast, blown sideways, in a thick fog of tiny flakes. "Oh my goodness." John looked out and shook his head.

"Does this mean no school on Monday, Daddy?" JJ was looking out the back door now.

"I doubt that, JJ. This time of year, that will be melted off by tomorrow afternoon." JJ looked crestfallen. John zipped up his heavy coat and braced himself for the cold.

"John?" Raliv touched John's shoulder. John stood now, a question in his eyes. "Do me a favor?"

"Anything, Pop."

"Could you stop by one night just to visit?"

"Yes, of course. Maybe Tina and the kids and I can all come next Saturday like today, bring lunch."

"I'd like that. A lot. I'd love to see Tina and the farm is a good place for the kids to burn off some energy." Raliv nodded. "But maybe one night, just you and me?"

John reached over and pulled Raliv close, hugging him for a long time. "Absolutely," he said into his father's ear. Then John pulled up his fur-lined hood, checked the coats of JJ and Becky, and, after hugs with Grandad, scurried them out into the car.

As he watched from the living room window, they drove down the long driveway, horn honking goodbye. Raliv had an almost overwhelming urge to cry, but this felt different. He didn't feel like crying because they were leaving or out of sorrow, at least not primarily, but he felt tears of happiness, because the visit from his son and grandchildren had made him so happy, just their being there, and being able to talk about Colleen. He realized he had almost forgotten what it felt like to be happy. It was such a revelation to know he could actually be happy, that it was okay to be happy, that he didn't have to feel like he was somehow betraying Colleen if he found some happiness in life.

After watching the car disappear into the snow, Raliv came back to look out the kitchen window, hoping to see smoke from the chimney of the cabin, but the cabin was too far away and there was too much snow at that. He worried about Pan. He hoped Pan was in the cabin, that they were safe.

Raliv went back into the living room to finish his wine. Felicity wandered out from the bedroom and circled the room before jumping into her master's lap and falling asleep.

Chapter 9

Raliv awoke late the next day. Just as he had feared, the extra cup of coffee had kept him awake, despite the second glass of wine he had enjoyed after John and the grandchildren had left. He had tried watching television, but it didn't hold his attention. He kept flipping through the channels and scrolling along the on-screen guide until he realized he was not truly actually reading the titles but simply watching the screen flip from station to station.

Turning off the television, he read in the novel he was well into, which did hold his attention, but still he did not feel drowsy. Recalling he had squirreled away the recorder in the nightstand, he retrieved that and played, sitting on the edge of the bed, for a long time. He had only figured out the three songs, so after he had played each of them through a number of times, he decided to branch out. He remembered a song called "El Condor Pasa," a Peruvian song often played on a traditional pan flute, but decided to give it a try on his recorder.

He and Colleen had come across Andean folk music groups on their travels several times, and this was one of her favorites. They had always enjoyed buying CDs from street musicians and playing them later at home, reliving the days and places they had visited. He tried to recall the melody.

The only words he knew were Paul Simon's so he recited the lyrics in his head as he picked out the first part of the melody.

"I'd rather be a turtle than a snail . . ." He played it repeatedly until he had that part memorized a little, then went for the high part. "If I could . . ." Felicity jumped up on the bed and tried to rub her cheek on Raliv's arm as he played. Was that appreciation or "please stop," he wondered. It was after midnight when he had finally wound down, whispered to the empty side of the bed, "Good night, sweetheart," glanced up at the dreamcatcher just to remind himself it was there, and gone to sleep.

He had slept fitfully too, awakening several times in the night which made him recall the dreams he was having, dreams about needing to find his classroom to teach, but he was unfamiliar with the layout of the school and seemed perpetually stranded on a stairwell, and others dreams about trying to run across empty fields but being caught in a sluggish slow-motion crawl that he could not break out of despite his attempts.

Finally, Felicity had strolled up Raliv's body in the bed again this morning, stopping now to smell his breath, perhaps checking to see why he was not already awake and petting her. "Okay, okay, I'm up." Raliv turned over and the calico jumped to the floor. Raliv sat up in bed now and looked at the cat. *That cannot be a pleasant smell*, he thought, *my breath first thing in the morning*.

The bed was tossed and messy from his restless sleep. He straightened the covers and smoothed out the bed, not really made but neat enough. He glanced again at the dreamcatcher and shrugged, as if to say, "Where were you?" He was halfway through his morning routine in the bathroom when he looked at the simple wall clock there and saw it was already nine o'clock. He began to hurry his pace, although he certainly had nothing on his agenda for today.

Then he remembered the snow and opened the blind to look out the window. The brightness was blinding. The sun was out but everything was covered with snow. The holly tree had a white coating on the top. Long icicles hung from the gutter, already dripping. The road back to the cabin was only a treeless path through the snow, punctuated by the two-tone silhouettes of the Rose of Sharon bushes at the back of the yard. Everything was white or some shade of white. And the sun was gleaming off of it. John was right; it would be melting off quickly.

Now Raliv began to hurry with purpose. He loved being in the woods when it snowed, with everything hushed by the blanket of crystals. He simply had to get to the woods before it was all melted off. He filled Felicity's water dish, scooped the litter, checked the feeder, washed up, then hurried back to the bedroom to dress.

This would take a little thinking. It was cold now, but soon would be warmer and much wetter. He decided layers of clothes were in order so he could peel off layers as it warmed. He rubbed a thin layer of liniment on his back and put on another tired tee shirt, this one with an iguana on it that had the words "Pura Vida" printed on the back. It was from the trip they had made together to Costa Rica, but the shirt was nearly threadbare now. He added layers, first a light sweatshirt, then a heavier work shirt. He decided to wear the canvas pants he had bought at the bargain bin at the hardware store. They were a bit stiff, but were waterproof, and that would be welcome.

Raliv stood in the kitchen, munching on a protein bar and waiting for the drip maker to finish brewing his morning cup. He decided the parka hanging by the back door from yesterday was too heavy, so he went to hang it up.

The pewee picture fell out of the pocket and fluttered to the floor. He reached over and picked it up. His back was already much better. He had meant to share the drawing with John but had forgotten all about it. He put the drawing on the counter next to the phone to show John when he saw him.

Then he felt the cell phone still in another pocket. He took it out and checked the charge. It was still fine. There were no new messages and no missed calls, but then, Raliv supposed he would need to send messages or make a call if he hoped to receive any. He decided he needed to carry the phone, since in snowy conditions, who knew what could befall Raliv out in the woods? It was even harder to see the various holes and tangles in the snow, and footing in the ice, snow, and, later, mud was of course an issue. And when Raliv made it to the top of the hill above the cabin, the path he had already mapped out for himself in his head, the signal was strong enough to call out, if he needed to. He put the phone on the table while he hung up the parka and retrieved a lighter coat, a windbreaker he often used as a raincoat. With the layers beneath, it should be plenty.

He tried to decide if he should retrieve his .22 from the safe but didn't really want to head into the forest with that mindset, the idea of hunting something, and he didn't want to have to worry about carrying the weight of the gun. The walk would be more laborious because of the snow and having to tote the gun would only add to that. Besides, he had plenty of food from the market he had just shopped at earlier in the week. No, he just wanted to take a walk through the woods while the snow was still there. It was that simple.

Except, there was something more. He also wanted to see if Pan had stayed in the cabin. He needed to check on Pan and know they were safe. But now that his thoughts turned to Pan, what could Raliv take as a gift today? Now that he had realized he needed to be aware of his guest's living circumstances, that they were someone who lived off the land and evidently needed very little, he wanted to be thoughtful about what might be appropriate. He gazed out the window as he mulled it over. The scene outside was still completely white. The coffee was giving its last few gurgles of water through the spout.

Fruit. How could Pan have any sort of fruit this time of year, especially with the hard freeze and now this blanket of snow? Raliv reached into the pantry and pulled out a mesh bag that had once had onions in it and put two oranges, a tangerine, and an apple in it, then held it up and decided that was too little, so he went the fridge and pulled out some carrots and several stalks of celery.

Fresh produce would be something Pan probably got too little of, especially in a snowstorm. But the cold snap would have impacted Pan's options as well, having no shelter to store things in, at least as far as Raliv could discern. But whoever Pan was, they didn't seem like a homeless person, exactly. They had not asked for a thing, and, in fact, seemed quite at home living in the woods. Quite the opposite of homeless, Pan seemed completely at home wherever they were. Raliv pulled a twist tie from a drawer and closed the top of the mesh bag tightly.

Where was Pan sleeping when he wasn't at the cabin, if he had stayed in the cabin at all? Raliv had walked every inch of the farm and knew every place on it. There were no caves on the land, no rock outcropping to provide shelter. They might have a tent, but a tent draws attention, and has to be put up and taken down, and Pan clearly did not seek attention and seemed more mobile than even a tent would suggest.

Probably an A-frame, Raliv decided. Maybe down near the creek where the land flattened out, Pan had built a simple shelter from boughs of pines, covering it with leaves and more pine branches. There were plenty of pine trees down there, and plenty of pine straw to make a bed from. The creek water was clean. It would be a welcome spot for a traveler. But Pan had not been on Raliv's farm for very long, he didn't think. They traveled. So where was Pan from? Where would they go from here? And when? Raliv felt himself stiffen.

He didn't like thinking about Pan leaving, even though he knew it was no doubt inevitable. He liked having Pan there on the farm. There was a certain comfort level in knowing Pan was there, helping Raliv keep an eye on things. A farm can be a lot to watch by himself, not that he had any livestock or cropland to tend. But being the steward of the land was still plenty.

The coffee maker beeped that it was finished, shaking Raliv from his thoughts. He poured the hot water from his thermos that he had preheated it with and filled it full of the steaming black coffee. Then he sat at the kitchen table to write his note to Pan, but decided he wanted to see if they had stayed in the cabin first. Once he knew Pan was safe and okay, then he could write them a note out at the cabin.

Then he realized that it was possible Pan might still be at the cabin, for all he knew. Did Raliv want to surprise them by showing up? It was Raliv's cabin, so he clearly had every right to be there, but if Raliv suddenly showed up, would it scare Pan away? Would they run off and not come back? Whoever it was, they clearly valued privacy even more than Raliv did.

Raliv did not want to frighten Pan away from the farm. The cabin had a back door. Raliv decided he would park his truck far enough away from the cabin and he would make sure to slam the door and make lots of noise so Pan could easily slip out the back door if they chose. And, who knew? Maybe Raliv would finally meet Pan in person.

Raliv put on his windbreaker, slid the phone in one pocket and zipped it closed, then decided he wanted to take the recorder out to the cabin. One of the main things Raliv loved about the woods in the snow was the quiet and now he wondered what the flute would sound like in the snowy woods. All the rest of the year, the birds and the wind in the trees sang to him. Perhaps now he could serenade an owl sleeping on a black gum branch on a very bright, wintry day. He returned to the bedroom, got the little instrument, put it in another pocket, and headed for the backdoor.

He juggled the fruit and the thermos outside. There was a wet chill in the air, but it was already warmer than it had been yesterday. The snow would not last very long. He climbed into the truck, slid the fruit and thermos onto the bench seat next to him, put the key in, and turned it. The starter moaned, then clicked quickly. The tired old battery was no match for the cold the day before, he realized.

He sat there for a moment trying to decide the best way to jump the battery, but he knew it was a bad plan: jump the battery, then drive out into the woods and hope it was charged up enough by then to restart. It was just not a good idea. He could be stranded out there, and then he would have to climb up the hill and call John to come out and help him on a Sunday, or maybe Mr. Phelps up the road, but either way, he would be putting someone out simply by not thinking this through.

He knew what he had to do. He needed to take Colleen's

little SUV out of the garage and use it. But that was depending on it starting also, since he had not driven it for at least a couple of months. It needed to be run, and, besides, his pickup was awful in snow, the rear-wheel drive and the lighter weight of the back end resulting in lousy traction. Colleen's car had front wheel drive, which would be much better.

The garage was detached from the house and was several yards beyond where anyone ever parked. Raliv lifted the two-by-four from the slot that held the two wooden doors closed. He swung one door open, the snow pushing back from the drive, then opened the other peeling white door.

There was Colleen's car, well, their car, but she had done her usual deep research, finding on the web the cars that were well-rated then finding one listed online at a price she was confident she could bring down to the level she was willing to pay. When it came to big purchases, Colleen loved doing the research. And she had taken great care of the car, keeping it uncluttered, for the most part, and running it through the car wash whenever they drove into the city. She had even kept the oil change register up to date.

He and Colleen had both adhered to the philosophy of keeping a car for a long time rather than switching every few years. If they were going to keep the car and make sure it lasted, they needed to maintain it well, she had believed. And now, it was his car.

Raliv pressed the key fob button and the doors unlocked and the parking lights came on, although why he had locked it in the garage was not clear to him just now, force of habit, he supposed. So far, so good. Raliv put the bag of fruits and vegetables in the back seat, then slid into the front seat, leading with the thermos. Even after losing so much weight, it took a little sucking in of the belly to get in since the building was barely a single car garage.

He pushed the key in and turned it and the car started up immediately. Then he remembered it had heated seats, which Colleen had insisted upon, so he pressed the button to turn on the seat warmer. He backed out carefully. Once he had cleared the garage doors, he debated closing the doors but decided he was burning too much time on trivial matters.

Out in the driveway, the brightness of the sun blinded Raliv. He wished he had brought his sunglasses. He should have anticipated he would be snow blind. Retrieving Colleen's sunglasses from the overhead compartment, he put on her oversized, round, black-and-white striped glasses and headed towards the cabin. It wasn't like he would be seeing anyone, and, even if he did, what would they care what sunglasses he had on, as long as his eyes were protected. Before he reached the opening in the ruined barbed wire fence, he had to turn down the seat warmer. Now that, he decided, was a great invention.

When he drove across the meadow, Raliv could see the message chair was still snow-covered. Pan had not been there yet. Raliv hoped they were okay. *People do die from exposure*, he thought. If Pan had been too stubborn or too shy to go to the cabin, it could have been bad. He tried to imagine someone staying warm in a pine-branch A-frame in the cold and snow, although the A-frame was only his supposition, after all.

He drove across the field and into the forest. Driving back the narrow path was as much from memory as it was anything, since the snow made everything look the same. By the time he pulled onto the yard of the cabin, the car was warm. He liked Colleen's car. It had done great in the snow and the few places that were already muddying up. He made a mental note to drive it into the city next week and wash the mud and grime off that this trip would leave on it. He parked farther out than he planned and made a point of slamming the car doors when he got out, after he retrieved the mesh bag. He trudged to the door with his thermos and his gift, pulled open the screen, and pushed the heavy front door open.

Inside, the cabin was still vaguely warm. Pan had stayed. Raliv felt a sigh of relief. It wasn't exactly toasty in the cabin, but it would have been far colder if there had been no fire. Raliv took off Colleen's sunglasses and put them in the pocket with the recorder. He glanced at the bed and saw it looked exactly like Raliv had left it. In fact, it did not look like it had been slept in at all.

At his feet, on the rag rug, the woven blanket they kept draped over the footboard was folded neatly with the throw pillows stacked on top. "You slept on the floor?" Raliv said aloud, and his voice filled the cabin. He shook his head. That was why he had made the bed, for Pan to have a nice comfortable place to sleep. But maybe, if you were used to sleeping on the ground outside on pine straw under dry leaves, a rag rug and a couple of pillows was as much luxury as you would seek. He checked out the fireplace. He could tell it had been used from the cool, damp, smoky smell. Then he glanced at the pile of firewood he kept inside to keep it dry and the pile was twice as high as it had been. Raliv stepped past the wood to the backdoor.

Outside, the pile of split wood was as tall as Raliv. Pan had split all the logs from the poplar tree. Raliv winced just a little and felt his back with one hand, which did not hurt right now, but even his back seemed able to imagine what it would feel like to split that much wood in one setting. He had hurt himself doing less than a fourth of that much work.

Raliv came back inside. "I'd say I got the better part of this deal, huh, sweetie?" He glanced now at the photo on the mantle and realized it had been moved. Not moved, exactly, turned ever so slightly, as one would do if you picked it up to study it and put it back down. He stood there for a moment, thinking. That would be the first time Pan had any idea about who Colleen was, who it was Raliv grieved, and what she looked like. Obviously, Pan saw Raliv's sorrow, his mourning, but now, Pan knew just who it was for. It didn't feel intrusive, exactly. Raliv had invited Pan in. Rather, it felt more like letting someone in on a secret, not that everyone didn't already know about Colleen. But this was different. This was someone new, someone who never met Colleen, holding her picture, looking at the two of them on the beach, happy, close, and, in Raliv's view, obviously deeply in love. He was glad Pan had looked at the photo. He hoped

Pan understood why it had been so hard to move forward, so difficult to find some way to make sense of it all.

But even now, and it had only been a few months, Raliv was finding a kind of footing. He had loved having John and the grandchildren over and telling the stories about Nana and Grandad. And he was enjoying doing some cooking now. He had always loved cooking with Colleen before, but he had found cooking alone, only for himself, to be onerous at first. And he liked playing the recorder. In fact, he was surprised at just how much he was enjoying that and maybe even more surprised that he seemed to have a bit of a knack at it, although that was perhaps more due to repetition than innate skill. Still, he was able to pick out the songs.

Raliv walked over and adjusted the picture, which immediately struck him as odd, since he really hadn't positioned it in any particular way before. He went over to the table, removed the steel cup lid from the thermos, and poured himself some coffee. He wanted to take a walk, but first things first. He sat for a moment, sipping the coffee, looking around the cabin, which was always a peaceful spot but was now deafeningly quiet with the snow muffling every whisper of sound outside. The light coming through the window above the bed refracted off the geode, sending a sliver of sunbeam across the floor.

Raliv took another drink of coffee and decided to build a small fire in the cookstove. It was safer than one in the fireplace if he wasn't around, and Raliv figured he would be wet and cold when he came back from his hike. He would only build a little fire, just enough to take the chill off and to have some coals to add to when he came back. The cookstove was tepid. There had been a fire in it the night before. He wadded up a grocery store ad that had come in the mail and put it in the center of the firebox, then placed a pinecone he had coated with candle wax from one of Colleen's used up scented candles. Then he teepee'd some kindling around that and lit a match to the paper.

The fire started up quickly. He let it burn some to let the wood catch, drank some more coffee, then added a few larger pieces of wood. That should last until he came back. He closed the door and adjusted the air flow vents. Then he wondered just what Pan had done for supper?

What had Pan eaten here, if they had even eaten? Raliv swigged down the last of the coffee he had poured and walked over to the pantry. Everything inside looked in order as far as he could tell. Had Pan eaten some sardines or maybe some Vienna sausages? Raliv didn't keep track of his reserves with enough detail to know from glancing at the shelves. He looked into the recycling bag and saw an empty, rinsed-out pork and beans can. "Really?" Raliv looked back in the sack. "Pork and Beans?" He shook his head in dismay, then saw the vegetable oil on the wrong shelf. Colleen would never have put the oil with the canned soup. So Pan had cooked something more. He was glad. A rabbit, some fish, what would have been for supper? The thought of it made Raliv's stomach growl.

Enough sleuthing, he decided. Time to take his walk. He would walk up the hill through the woods, just as he planned, then take the power line path and end up coming to the message chair from the other direction. He needed to write his note and get outside, before the snow was all gone. He half-sat, half-squatted at the desk, eager to get out the door.

```
Dear Pan,

    Thanks for cutting all that wood.
That was a lot of work. I can't believe
you slept on the rug. I made the bed up
just for you. I'm very glad you stayed
in the cabin. It makes me happy that
you are safe.

    I took your advice and had my son and
his family come visit. It was wonderful.
It was maybe the best I have felt since
```

Colleen passed away. I realize now how much I want to talk about her. She was my very best friend, my sweetheart, my companion, my whole world. She is gone now, but I know, having had her love for all those years, I am truly a lucky man.

Here are some fruits and vegetables I thought you might enjoy. I'm guessing fruit is hard to find around here just now.

Raliv

He folded up the note and put it in another zip top bag, slid it into a pocket, and headed out the door with the produce in one hand. Outside, it was still bright, but the dripping from the edge of the cabin told him the melting was on. He pulled the door shut, put on the black-and-white striped sunglasses and headed up the hillside.

In the woods, it was every bit as quiet as he had expected it to be. It was quiet and peaceful and almost mystical in its starkness. Snow fell off of branches high above him, melting, leaving shallow holes in the white floor of the forest. He made his way slowly, because he didn't want to lose his footing, but also because he simply was where he meant to be.

He climbed several yards, then stopped to look around him, enjoying the wintery scene. This was always something he did without Colleen. She could appreciate a good snowstorm, but always from the warmth of the inside. Looking out a window at the snow was fine with her. Besides, she had a habit of stepping into holes and tripping over branches, which also took the fun out of it for her. But she had encouraged Raliv to go ahead and take a walk, to be careful, and to enjoy himself.

Pan and the Message Chair

He trudged now towards the top of the hill. He was almost to the spot where he had first seen Pan's snare set. He looked around now to see if there was another, but all the branches were pulled down by the weight of the snow, although none, as far as he could tell, was set as a trap. But there were lots of tracks in the snow: rabbits, squirrels, and a raccoon looked to have passed through. The two-footed hop of a wren wound around a fallen red oak. But it was quiet. Even the snow falling off the branches seemed to be doing so in as quiet a manner as possible, as if not to disturb the eerie silence. He stopped next to a shagbark hickory to catch his breath and to just take in the scenery.

Then he remembered about playing his recorder in the quiet, just to hear the sound of it. He put the fruit down, unzipped the pocket of his windbreaker, and took out the recorder and began playing "Au Clair de la Lune." His fingers were a little cold, and the gloves made the instrument feel different, but he had played it so many times by now, he played it through without trouble.

He wasn't sure what he expected, but the flute-y tune had floated in the cool air smoothly, clearly. Had he thought the snow would swallow up the sound the way it had swallowed up the ground? One difference was that there was no echo. Many times in the woods, Raliv had trouble telling what direction a sound had originated from because the trees acted as echo spots, but his melody had been stark and clean in the woods. He gave himself a smile, happy with the little experiment of playing a song back to his neighbors. He put the recorder away again, picked up the produce, and climbed the final few yards to the power line path.

He wasn't sorry to leave the woods. He liked being out in a field all alone after a snow just as much as being in the woods and, besides, the walking was easier. Johnson grass seed heads bowed gently, the snow already off of them. The snow had crusted over some here in the sunlight, melting into a thin sheet of ice atop the few inches of snow beneath.

Raliv crunched along slowly, but deliberately, following the line to where it turned and opened up onto the meadow. The message chair was there, the snow off the seat. It would not have melted off completely yet, so Raliv knew Pan had been there. He resisted the urge to quicken his pace. He wanted to see what was there. He had already received a great gift of split wood, so he didn't expect anything along those lines, but he did want to get the message from Pan. First, he wanted to enjoy what he was doing and not hurry through it.

By the time Raliv made it to the chair, he was ready to sit. Walking cross-country in snow always took more energy. There was a note there, folded neatly and wedged into the slot they usually used. Some snow from the top of the backrest had melted water onto the note, making it damp, but it wasn't soggy yet. He sat at the chair, put the mesh bag beside him on the seat, carefully unfolded the note and read it.

Dear Raliv,

Thank you for letting me stay in your cabin. It was perfect, beautiful, and a luxury for me. I am indebted to you. It was bad outside last night.

You ask for a friend, but I think you have many more friends than you realize. They will be there for you whenever you are ready for them, whenever you need them. They know all the places you have been and they will be there when you arrive wherever you are going. Your friends are holding you up even now, even if you don't see it. That is what friends do. They hold you up, even if your arms are not reached out. They hear you, even when you don't speak.

Pan and the Message Chair

I am glad to be

Your friend,

Pan

Raliv sat there for a long while, reading and re-reading the note, looking off at the osprey nest where the two birds were huddled in, gazing down the hillside where the row of trees just budding outlined the way to the beaver pond. He was being watched again. He knew it. But all he saw was the grey-black tree trunks and the backdrop of white that was already beginning to show some leaves poking through as the snow melted.

After a while, Raliv began retracing his steps to return to the cabin. In the open, his steps were still visible where he had made his way to the chair, but in the woods, much of the snow was melting away now. He moved more quickly now, going downhill and being ready to get warm. He made his way to the cabin, stoked up the fire in the cookstove, poured the remaining coffee in his thermos into the steel cup, and sat in his tired chair to enjoy his second cup.

Raliv looked at Colleen's chair, then up at the photo. "I made a new friend today, Honey. You met them last night. Remember? Pan. What did you think?" He smiled and took a drink of coffee.

Raliv stayed in the cabin until after lunch, which consisted of a can of sardines in hot sauce and a small can of fruit cocktail, which he drank down as much as ate. He had built a fire in the cookstove, but he had not built it up enough to cook anything, and, what's more, other than oats, rice, or beans, there really was nothing much to cook.

By the time he had closed off the vent, the fire was spent, and he was ready to go back to the farmhouse. Outside, the light was getting that faded low angle of the sun look, and he wanted to get back before dark, since he knew it would be muddy and, perhaps, tricky where the mudpuddles always formed. But the car did fine, spinning some mud on the fenders, but otherwise navigating the path easily.

He parked the car in the driveway and came inside, where Felicity came running up to rub against his leg. Emptying his pockets onto the kitchen table, he then took the layers of clothes off in the hallway next to the laundry room. He tossed it all into the washing machine, added the heavy clothes from the hamper, and started the wash.

It wasn't late yet, certainly not supper time, so Raliv stood in the hallway with only his boxer shorts on, trying to decide what to do. Then he nodded his head and went to the kitchen and pulled a bottle of beer from the refrigerator. Passing the table, he picked up the cellphone. He went into the bathroom and started running very warm water in the tub. He hadn't taken a bath in a long time, usually opting for the efficiency of a shower. A long soak in a hot tub with a good beer seemed just the ticket. It would be something different. He usually only drank beer with his pals on their occasional fishing trips, but today, a beer sounded tasty.

As he waited for the tub to fill, he pressed the home button on the phone then opened the app to send messages. They were all from weeks before, both messages to Raliv and some to Colleen. He found the message stream from his old friends in his hometown, reread the friendly jibes and joking, the pleasant banter that they had maintained through some fifty years of friendship. Then Raliv began typing with his thumb. "Hey, guys. Wondered if anyone wanted to meet up for lunch or something." He pressed send, put the phone on the counter next to the sink, and climbed into the tub. The water felt warm and relaxing and the beer was malty. This felt good and calm and luxurious.

His cellphone started beeping, the sound of messages coming through.

Chapter 10
Pan

Pan had spent the day gathering materials for the dreamcatcher. The little bead-like fossils were plentiful along the creek. The leather he had already tanned and now only needed to cut into thin strips with his knife, using a rotting log as a cutting board. He looped and tied until the dreamcatcher was finished.

He had made it small, smaller than he had once made them with the woman. They had made them together to sell along the roadside, a few dollars that helped with food and the barest of necessities, the sort of necessities he now did without. Perhaps they weren't truly necessary, but they still did not feel like luxuries. Soap, toiletries, matches, salt for curing meats.

Raliv had asked him what he needed, and the truth was, he needed almost nothing. Was that a kind of wealth? He had once asked for more and been disappointed when he could not find it, when he had received more, but then it was withdrawn. It was a kind of cruel joke people played on each other, to be there and then not be, to care and then not care.

Pan decided the lack of need was of greater value to him than too much of what he didn't need. But maybe that was not fair either. Maybe he did desire a few things. There was companionship, even the kind of coming together he and Raliv had, these notes and gifts. It felt good to share again. It had been so long and he had known the kind of solitude where he had to speak his thoughts aloud just to hear the human voice and take whatever meager solace there was in hearing himself speak.

When the dreamcatcher was finished, Pan held it up. He nodded. "Not bad, Pan," he said aloud, his voice scratchy and hoarse. He had meant it as a kind of joke with his new name, but it reminded him. How long had it been since he had spoken? He put the gift down and started writing a note to Raliv.

Pan had nothing, which suited him fine. He could not lose something he did not have. But Raliv had so much more and Pan knew the old man could not lose what he had. He would not heal if he suffered more loss. Raliv was curious about the geode, but there wasn't much to tell. Or there was too much to go into: Pan's son, the letter, the woman he had met and come to know.

Karen.

He had not allowed himself to even think her name for a long time. Karen, although she, like Pan, had gone by lots of different names, and sometimes just said whatever came to mind as her name. She told a farmer they were buying brown eggs from that her name was Raccoon, because she loved eggs, she had told Pan later. When their camp had been discovered by hikers with brightly colored day packs and fancy hiking shoes, she had introduced herself as Rainbow and Pan as Grey Wolf. When the hikers had left after sharing some trail mix with the two of them, she had explained she was inspired first by their too bright clothing and then decided he himself looked like a grey wolf with his grey beard and hair, a very tired, old grey wolf. She laughed that small chuckle she had when she said it. She had helped him when he needed help.

Pan wanted to help Raliv and hoped maybe he was. It had been a long time since he had helped anyone. He didn't harm anyone, and he just kept to himself. If everyone kept to themselves, it might solve a lot of the problems in the world. But that wasn't right either. Helping Raliv was helping himself, wasn't it? If he had known grief, wasn't he in a better position to reach out to the old man? He didn't know any special secrets about grieving, but he knew what it felt like and maybe that was enough. What could he give the old man that might help? What did Raliv need? It probably wasn't something material, maybe just being engaged.

A cold wind was blowing in from the north. Pan added more layers of pine boughs and leaves to his hut. He had slept in cold before, but it was never good to get too cold. He made his way along the other side of the tree line and came out into the old pasture from the back side of the pond. Walking made him warmer, but he could feel the moisture in the air, the cold.

He put the dreamcatcher and note under a pebble so they would not blow away then stepped back into the trees, watching from behind a tall eastern white pine that swayed in the growing wind. He hid from Raliv's sight and from the cold wind. The pine branches swung around him in a kind of embrace. The scent of the tree surrounded him. He had stood for several moments and the warmth from walking was gone when he heard the truck chugging along the ridge road.

Raliv stopped the truck but left it running, then half-stepped, half-fell out of the truck. He was bent over, walking like a suddenly much older version of himself. Pan had heard the sound of wood chopping taking place the previous day, so it was not hard to guess what had happened. Pan was shivering now, making standing still much harder, but Raliv didn't seem to be looking around for him today. Pan was glad for that, although the bushy tree provided lots of hiding space. He watched Raliv pick up the dreamcatcher, hold it there for a moment, then leave a bag and stumble back across the little garden area and into the truck. Pan had to walk around the tree in concert with the passing of the truck to remain hidden.

After the truck had growled away, Pan walked over to the chair. The bag had fishing line and hooks in it. He looked over at the little pond where small ripples were being blown across by the cold wind. That would work. And he knew how he would make that work.

He read the note, then reread it. He was helping the old man.

How different it felt to have Raliv open up to him, tell him about his need for love and to love. It was a universal need, of course, but one many people feel odd expressing, especially to someone they really don't know. It is a vulnerability that most people avoided. It was one Pan himself avoided, had been avoiding for a long time, perhaps too long. Pan wondered just then who might be left of the people he had known. Who could he tell, he wished he had love?

There were some: he knew that. There was his sister and also his old best friend, if they were still around, and maybe even his ex-wife, if she had ever come back. The thought caught him up and he shook his head and marched straight across the field and into the valley below, not worrying about staying hidden. The old man was now safe in his house and wouldn't be coming back. His note said it was supposed to get even colder. Pan did not like the sound of that. He gathered chickweed and wild onions along the side of the meadow. He needed more fuel.

Back at his camp, he built a small fire using a big stone to block the wind. The trees danced slowly, gracefully in the wind. He boiled a broth of quail bones and giblets. While it cooked, Pan took the saved lid of the sardine can and folded it back and forth along several vertices until he had a shape of a crude fishing spoon in his hand. He smoothed the edges along a sandstone rock, then punched holes in either end with the tip of his knife. He tied on a hook, then knotted it onto a longer line.

He drank and ate his broth and munched on the greens he had picked. Then he hiked to the bamboo stand where he cut a long pole. Later that afternoon, he waved the pole along the edge of the pond. The fish were small, but very eager to attack the little silver lure he had crafted. He had made a stringer from some of the twine Raliv had given him and before long had plenty of fish for dinner and some more to keep in the little stream, wriggling along in the current still attached to the string.

He cleaned several fish, little bluegill, skewering and

cooking them over the fire. He ate them with curly dock leaves he had found near the beaver pond and tossed into the pot. He was not tempted to stay outside late. If the hut was no palace, it at least would protect him from the wind. With the large rock he had used as his fire brace now pulled into the middle of his shelter, he climbed inside, filling in the opening with more leaves from inside, pine branches he had cut and placed inside, and finally his rucksack.

Pan wore every piece of his clothing to build layers, although he had only a few articles and what he had was in tatters. He wrapped himself up in his blankets. It promised to be a difficult night, but he had seen this kind of weather before. He would be okay. He curled up in the shelter and tried to sleep, thinking first about Karen, then about his son.

As soon as he heard the first chipping sparrow call, Pan climbed out of his hut and started his fire again. He felt a chill deep into his core that he knew would take days to overcome. He pulled the stone back out of his shelter to reheat it for this night, since there was nothing about the early morning cold that promised warmer weather. He made a fishbone broth and drank it down.

His warmed breath was a cloud before him, and tiny ice crystals formed in his beard. He knew what to take to Raliv. He had his medicine for pulled muscles he had made in the fall stored in a plastic water bottle found alongside a road somewhere. And he had the little clay pot he had made up in the mountains when he had found a large swathe of clay along a creek and had fired it in a pit kiln using a shale glaze. Most of the pots he had made broke apart as they cooled but a few had survived. It wasn't a pretty pot, but it was functional for the job.

He rummaged through his sack, his fingers awkward and stiff from the bitter wind. His hands were shaky from being so cold. If he had another pair of socks, he would put them on as mittens, but it was probably easier to warm his hands before the fire than his feet.

He thought about what he would write to Raliv. He needed

to tell the old man that he had lots of love. It was obvious just looking around him. Everywhere, there was evidence of the love he had had with his wife. That she was gone did not change that. It was the same with Pan, he thought now. He still had the love of his son. All of this, all of the travels, it was evidence of the love.

He had camped with his son many times, even after he was grown and had been off to the military. They still camped and hunted and fished. The camping they had done was not like Pan was doing now, exactly, although that was when the two of them had started learning about survival skills. It was because of all the trips, all the adventures they had together, that his son had decided to become a ranger. He had, in a sense, been training for it his entire life.

So if Pan gathered fiddlehead ferns for a meal, that in itself was not only honoring the memory of his son, but also keeping his son's love forever around him. Pan had taught his son everything he could about the outdoors, but in the end, it was the son who excelled at it in every way. Pan now pictured his son, so tall and agile and strong, poised with a spear in an atlatl he had made himself, ready to take the barking squirrel in a single fluid motion. He smiled a small, stiff smile at the picture in his head. Had he gotten the squirrel? Just now, he didn't recall, and it really didn't matter.

He was pulling out the liniment when he came across the letter again. This time, he took it out and unfolded it. He knew it by heart, of course, although he had not read it in a long time. He opened it and read the opening line: "Regret to inform you" . . . Pan looked up, away from the letter, into the forest where birds were starting to take up the morning song despite the cold. There, in the stand of sycamores and poplars, stood his son. There, along the tiny stream where the fish kept from yesterday were resting on the bottom, his son kneeled to check their wellbeing. The evidence. He folded up the letter and placed it carefully back into the rucksack.

Pan huddled closer to the fire. He placed his shivering

fingers over the flames to loosen them so he could write a note. As stiff as his fingers were now, he wasn't sure he could write legibly. He let his mind wander. Who would still be in his hometown? He hoped they were safe. His hometown, Wylers Ford, was so far away now, down in a valley by a river he and his son had fished so often. He wondered where Karen was. His fingers were warmer now so he wrote a note, sharing with the old man what he himself had come to know, that everyone carries the love with them that they have built and all they need to do is ask. Why didn't he himself ask? Maybe he would.

Then he made his way through the trees to the meadow. He had heard the truck earlier, heading back to the cabin. He left the note and the liniment, then hid, shivering, behind the pine tree. It provided less protection today than it did the day before from the cold. This was miserable, Pan thought.

He had not been hiding long when the shuddering truck came across the field. Raliv climbed out of the truck, shuffled quickly over to the chair, picked up the baggy with the liniment and note in it, hustled as quickly as a man with a sore back probably could, and drove off. The old man was going someplace warm. Pan wondered why he had even ventured out on such a day.

There was only a note this time. That was okay. He had said he didn't need anything, and he had meant it. He stood in the growing cold and read the note. Raliv was inviting Pan to stay in the cabin. Pan wouldn't go, but it was such a generous offer. And he had answered Pan's question.

Pan looked up across his shoulder in the direction of the farmhouse. He was Raliv's friend. Who but a friend would share his cabin with Pan? Maybe he would go to the cabin. It was so bitterly cold. And snow? Pan walked across the field, gathering his feet as he went into a trot. The running felt good. At his camp, he grabbed his rucksack and the stringer of fish and worked his way towards the cabin. Yes, to be warm would feel so good. He hoped he was as good a friend to Raliv.

Stepping into the cabin out of the wind was immediately better. He had cleaned the fish by the beaver pond and now carried them over to the sink. He rummaged in the cabinets and found a bowl to put them in. It was white with a picture of The Eiffel Tower in black lines across it. Then he stopped to look around him.

The small cabin was homey and cozy. The geode sat on the windowsill above the bed. He walked around the small room. There were the chairs, the brown leather one had to be where the old man sat. On the mantel, there was the picture. Pan picked it up and looked at it. It was a good picture, he thought. They certainly seemed to be well suited for each other, and happy in a gentle, genuine way.

Pan replaced the photo on the mantel and started a fire in the cookstove. The split wood caught easily and although he was not inclined to make a roaring fire and use up all the firewood, it already felt much better. It was strange to be in the old man's cabin without his being there too, as if he were being let in on someone's secrets without any words being exchanged. The bed was neatly made. There was the little desk, the small dining table. How many others had been allowed to enter what seemed to be a very personal space?

He wouldn't build a fire in the fireplace. That would use twice as much wood and Raliv had already hurt himself splitting logs. That's what Pan could do to repay Raliv. He could finish chopping the firewood up which would also warm his own deeply chilled core. He stoked up the fire a bit, then went outside and started splitting the chunks of maple.

In the cold, they split more easily, and once he got a rhythm going, he progressed through the pile quickly. He was taller than the old man, and that gave him more leverage to swing the axe.

Behind the cabin he saw the rain barrel sitting atop a platform making the top barely below the roof line. Running water. He went inside and washed his face and hands and then his arms up to his elbows in the frigid water from the spigot, but it felt so good to wash up the chill didn't matter. The little bar of soap that looked like it probably came from a hotel room somewhere was covered in soot and dirt after he finished washing so he rinsed it off well before putting it back. He didn't think the barrel running low would be an issue with all the rain they had had and with snow coming.

The cabin had warmed up nicely and Pan sat in one of the ladder-back chairs from the dining table. In the woods, he left as small a footprint as he could. He would do that here as well, of course. He would not sit in Raliv's chair, and certainly not in his wife's chair. Besides, he had been so very dirty up to his elbows, he could not imagine sitting anywhere that he might leave dirty. He would try to make it as if he had not even been there, except for the large pile of firewood, of course.

He reached over and dragged his rucksack closer and pulled out his recorder and played a soft melody, a lullaby he had learned to play for his son, but it was also one his former wife had frequently requested. He wondered how she had handled the news. He hoped she had done well. They had already been divorced when it happened, but a part of him wished he had been there for her, and maybe she for him.

As his body warmed, he felt his hunger grow. The cabin had a warm scent of wood smoke and it grew darker in the room. The darkening sky outside made evening come too early, so he lit the little oil lamp, found the vegetable oil, and fried up the fish. It had been a long time since he had fried anything, and it tasted very comforting to him. And there was salt and pepper. He cleaned his dishes in water from the heater at the end of the cookstove and replaced them where he had found them. Then he spread the blankets on the rug, extinguished the oil lamp, curled up, and slept as soundly as he had in many years, warm, full, safe.

Pan awoke to a very bright light shining through the window. He sat up and blinked. The cabin wasn't as warm as the night before, but it was still plenty warm for him. Outside, the world was white and gleaming. He stood and saw the pink band of light from the geode on the bedspread. He smiled.

Pan folded up the blankets and put them where he had slept, then hurried to gather the few things he had taken out of his bag. He didn't know when Raliv might come but he was certain he would. Maybe he should stay, meet Raliv face-to-face, have a conversation about anything, about what they enjoyed doing, about the outdoors that both of them obviously enjoyed, about family.

No, not family. Not just yet. No, he needed to go.

Pan hurried his pace. With the snow, food would be scarce, so he reached into the pantry and pulled out a can of beans. He opened the pull-back top and ate the beans from the can. There was no need to start a fire when he was leaving right away. He wondered if he could use the can. But maybe not leaving the evidence of his having helped himself to the beans, which Raliv had offered anyway, is a small deception, and Pan could not entertain such a thing with his new friend. He saw small cans of fruit cocktail and Vienna sausages, but he wouldn't take those. Pan lived off the land; he was no beggar and no thief. Before he left, he sat at the little desk and wrote a note to Raliv. Raliv had many friends, Pan included. He wanted to tell him so.

Pan had traveled only a few yards from the backdoor of the cabin when he heard the car door close in front of the cabin. He had not heard the truck and had nearly been caught crossing into the woods. He wasn't moving as quickly as he might have, stepping on various leafy patches that stuck up through the snow so as not to leave footprints. He made his way into the woods along the base of the hill and looked back at the cabin.

Raliv hadn't driven the truck. It was a car. That explained why Pan had not been warned by the rumbling truck. He would have to pay closer attention if Raliv started driving the SUV back and forth on the farm. Pan carried his bag over his shoulder, leaping and hopping from rock to log until he was finally far enough away from the cabin he figured he was not going to be discovered.

Then he heard the flute, a song floating down the hillside, muffled by the snow, but pretty. Pan stood very still, listening. The old man was good at playing the recorder, already as good or better than Pan, he would have to admit. Raliv was out hiking so that meant Pan needed to hurry. Pan listened for a while then tiptoed through the snow to the chair, brushing off what was left of the rapidly melting snow from the seat, and left his note. He hid amidst the poplar trees this time, blending in by not moving.

He had barely taken up his post when Raliv came lumbering up the hill from the other side, walking along a former power line opening. If Raliv had been interested, he could have followed the footprints left in the snow and probably traced where Pan was hiding, but he didn't seem to care.

Then Raliv left and Pan returned to the chair. Oranges. This was a luxury he had not had in many months. And celery, carrots. He ate a carrot while he read the note. Maybe Pan was helping. And maybe Raliv was helping Pan. He made his way back to his hut and gathered twigs for a fire. The hut itself looked like a giant snowball with sticks angled out awkwardly. He started a small fire, squatted next to it, then peeled a tangerine and ate it very slowly.

It was sweet and tart and delicious.

Chapter 11
Raliv

It was Monday and Raliv was moving around early. He had had a short evening, that had started well, but ended sadly. Two of his old friends were meeting him for lunch the following weekend, having set up the date to be at a barbecue joint they all recalled from the old days. Then, he had fixed a dinner of a porkchop heavily seasoned with herbs and baked with a thick slice of onion atop accompanied by a bowl full of crudités, and he had even found a show to watch on television. Then he sat in his chair with a small bowl of pecans to nibble and a one-finger pour of bourbon, watching the detective show on television.

He was doing fine. It was a program he and Colleen had watched earlier episodes and, as he often did, he figured out the culprit halfway through, being accustomed to the plotlines the writers used. He turned to Colleen's chair to share his revelation, and Raliv had lost the good evening to a bad night. He only wanted to share that the lead actor in the stage production where the murder took place was clearly the "perp," as they said in the show, that would soon be brought to justice by the deductive-thinking detective. But there was something in the familiar action of sharing his conclusion with Colleen, now lost, that sent him into a sad, long cry, even as he watched the ending of the program to see that he was correct. Felicity slept in Colleen's chair rather than Raliv's lap, as if his sorrow made his lap unwelcome.

When the show was over, Raliv switched to a music station on the television and sat in the living room, mostly dark except for the small table lamp beside him and the blue screen of the television, finishing his drink and wondering how he had ended up here again, grieving, waiting for something to change, so lorn he could hardly imagine a happy outcome even remotely possible.

He had retired to bed early, ready for the night to be done. Felicity followed him into the bedroom and slept in her little cat bed beneath the window, and Raliv had slid between the covers of the bed, glanced at the dreamcatcher, whispered again to the pillows beside him, "Good night, sweetheart. I love you," and lay in bed until sleep came.

Now it was morning, and Raliv sat at the kitchen table. It was such an ambush when the sorrow came out of something so innocuous as the innocent act of sharing, or rather, trying to share, something familiar, a simple expression of comfort and love between two people so meant for each other, so deeply in love they could almost read each other's thoughts.

But of course, that was it, in a nutshell. That was precisely what had overtaken him, the loss of the sharing, loss of the comfort of familiar actions as expressions of togetherness. He had made the regular coffee, his heart not being into the extra work of the espresso machine, slight though it was. He looked down at the bowl of cereal before him. He could barely remember the last time he had eaten a bowl of cereal, but it had been quick and easy and, besides, he had milk he should use up.

He ate slowly. Felicity wound herself around the table leg and Raliv's feet, purring. He needed a list. He needed a list of chores and menial tasks to help keep him busy and to not dwell on things. Was he only delaying the sorrow if he diverted his attention from it? Was it a sum-zero experience that he needed to suffer a certain quantity of debilitating sadness in order to recover, to find a way to progress in his life, to carry forward?

He would never stop missing Colleen. He knew that. But

he hoped he could, over time, as everyone said, learn to live in a new life, a new world, carrying the love they had built and nurtured and held so dear. But he didn't believe he had a quotient of grief he must endure. No, he was not denying his sorrow by focusing on chores and completing a list. He still felt it all. But he could not see how allowing himself to delve ever deeper into despair helped anything. Was that wrong?

The cereal was okay, a granola-esque, crunchy brand that at least he found filling. He had located it in the pantry, eye-level on the shelf below the top shelf, next to the oats – just where Colleen had placed it and would have told him he could find it. He took another bite.

Raliv stared out the window now as he chewed, the snow melted away except for a few icy remnants next to tree trunks, as if it had been nothing more than a small spill that had been swept up there and only awaited a dustpan for the final disposal. It would be gone before noon, he knew. The ground would be wet, so tilling the garden was out as a chore.

He needed to fix the key hook where it was attached to the wall, the one that had stripped out the drywall anchor. He had a whole variety of screw anchors gathered together over the years stashed away in an old tackle box converted for the storage of nuts and bolts and the like. It was only a matter of finding one a bit larger. And while he was at it, the row of pegs where everyone hung their coats when they came in was also loose, although, truth be told, Raliv found the coat rack to be too plain, too uninspired for his taste, but never mind that just now.

And he needed to run the vacuum cleaner as well. That should take up some time. He wrote the items on a pad of paper advertising for a video production company out west. He could do another load of laundry and the master bathroom was due a cleaning. He should check the hall bathroom too.

Then he remembered he had muddied up the backdoor area coming in from his hike in the woods the day before and wrote "Mop mudroom" on his list. It wasn't actually a mudroom, more of a mud foyer, since it really was only the area just inside the doorway that led into the kitchen from outside.

Colleen had wanted a piece of furniture to hang coats and pile boots under, but she had not found what she wanted exactly, although she had pointed out what she was looking for in magazines lots of times. It was just that the area available was too exact for any premade piece of furniture to fit right. The photos usually consisted of a bench to sit on so they could remove their boots without having to sit at a kitchen chair and thereby track the snow and mud across the room. There would be hooks above the bench for coats and jackets, and cubbyholes below the bench for the boots.

Raliv took another bite of cereal. He had a workshop out in the barn, and he had made some simple pieces for the house before at Colleen's request. There was the stand for the stereo in the third bedroom, now den, a room Raliv found little reason to enter these days. That had turned out fine and Colleen had fairly gushed over it. He had made the shelves for the pantry and they had turned out well too. He could try his hand at making the bench she had envisioned. But the first thing would be to find the pictures in the magazines she had shown him so he could draw it up.

This would be a bigger project, and a very visible one. If it were not carefully made, any flaws would be obvious to anyone else in the kitchen. Any fudged angle or uneven board would be easy to see against the lines of the room itself. And wasn't the kitchen where everyone seemed to gather? No, this was going to take a lot of patience and planning. He liked the idea. It was what he needed; a long-term, intricate project filled with lots of intermediate steps to keep him busy. He needed to keep busy. He took another spoonful of cereal and wrote on his list, "Find Magazines." That would be enough to jog his memory.

When his bowl was empty, he rinsed it out and loaded it and the spoon into the dishwasher. These days, it took him nearly a week to fill the dishwasher enough to run it. He searched in his mind's eye where the magazines might be. There was an ottoman in the living room that doubled as additional storage that Colleen kept some in. He might start there. There was a basket on Colleen's side of the bed that usually had a stack of magazines so thick it weighed the edges of the basket into a misshapen oval. There was a stack on the shelf by her desk in the den. He had lots of places to look, and he wasn't sure if he wanted to find the photo she had last shown him right away. It might be better if it took all day.

But if it took all day, he would miss going by the message chair. He had no need to head to the cabin just now, and frankly, the prospect of being in the cabin where he couldn't even talk on the phone seemed too lonely today. But he still wanted to head over and leave a message for Pan.

Pan claimed they were Raliv's friend, and although he knew so very little about Pan, Raliv welcomed the idea. It was perhaps the best kind of friend to have, someone who cared but who might also one day leave and not tell a soul anything that had been shared, a friend Raliv could just write anything to and not fear any kind of harsh reply. At least, Raliv didn't think there would ever be reason for Pan to rebuke him. They seemed wonderfully nonjudgmental. And Raliv had never said anything mean or hurtful to Pan. Why would he? He liked whoever Pan was, as odd as that sounded to him. No, he knew he was heading to the message chair at some point today, maybe sooner rather than later, since Raliv knew what he wanted to write to his new friend. It was about last night, and today. Yes, it was about all of it. He wanted to unload some of it, take some of it off his own mind.

Yes, he would see his old friends Jeff and Doug next week at lunch, but that would be different. Raliv wasn't sure this was a conversation for them, exactly. What he needed from these old friends was a reminder of the old days together as pals. What he wanted from them was a feeling of normalcy, a sense that everything somehow would be okay, without ever having to weigh it all down with his sadness. He wished the third friend, Jack, would be there but he was away. So it would be the three old friends, retelling old jokes, gently ribbing each other as they had for decades, the jibes themselves a part of the familiar patter of their conversations.

Raliv decided to start his search for the magazine in the den. That was where she often read her magazines, sitting in the huge chair she loved to snuggle down into. He sat at Colleen's desk chair before her desktop computer where she paid bills and kept up with her diverse range of friends through emails and social media. People took to Colleen naturally, her gentle wisdom, her quick wit, her ability to problem solve endearing her to even total strangers. She had friends all across the country, people they had met in travels who ended up telling Colleen their life stories while sitting at a table next to them at a beer garden somewhere and who later carried on long correspondences.

Raliv was leafing through the magazines on the shelf when he came across Colleen's legal pad where she kept up with the bills and recorded each month the amounts and figured how their accounts were doing. Colleen had liked knowing what was coming and liked planning, even for the unexpected, although what she really loved planning were their trips. He read down the page: electricity, water, internet, the usual entries. At the bottom was a notation for "vacation fund."

He looked up from the page. It had been her idea to set aside funds in a special account just for travel. There must be a pretty decent amount in there by now, since she had been deliberate about keeping up the deposits and even Raliv had remembered to transfer money into the account since he had had to take over. How much was there? Maybe a trip was something Raliv could plan, as well as the bench project.

Raliv pressed the buttons to turn on the screen and the computer and let the machine do its whirring while he continued flipping through the magazines. He paused to click the icon for the bank then returned to his scanning.

There it was.

There was the last picture Colleen had shown him of the bench she envisioned for the back entrance. It was simple enough looking, Raliv decided. He folded back the magazine and studied the photo. This one was only available in stores and was far too large for the spot they had beside the door, or the spot he had by the door, he corrected himself.

No, it was for her as well. He wanted to make this for Colleen as much as for himself. It was okay for this project to be for her as well. She was still very much part of his life. The computer gave out a plaintive beep and Raliv typed in the password. The screen changed colors and the accounts came up. Checking was what he expected, within twenty dollars or so. Savings was fine. Colleen insisted they keep some funds in a savings account, although the interest earned was so low as to make no difference at all. But the travel account was very healthy. Raliv felt his eyes widen. Yes, there was plenty in there for a trip. They had started talking about another trip before Colleen became so sick and here was the money for it. Where had they discussed?

They had talked about the beach for sure, and Raliv had wanted to take her one more time to the ocean. That was an idea. But they had also talked about another trip overseas, this time to eastern Europe, where they had not yet visited. Perhaps that was the best idea. Long days alone on the beach might not be as much a respite from his sorrow as traveling to another country, a new city.

Raliv exited the program and turned off the computer. He carried the legal pad and the magazine back into the kitchen. He flipped on the overhead light, the kitchen taking on a warm, cheery feel, put the magazine on the counter, and sat at the table with the pad of paper. He would plan his trip right here, right in Colleen's legal pad, where she enjoyed keeping all her thoughts and plans. He flipped the page over and started to write the year and the destination of his trip, but the blank page stopped him.

There would be a time to plan this trip, but he needed to write Pan first. Seeing the blank page had reminded him of his desire to write more than a mere note to his friend Pan. It was as if he needed to write it all out before he could really think about doing anything else. He wanted to tell Pan all about how hard this was, because maybe just writing it down would help Raliv take it out of himself, if even for a moment. He clicked the pen and began writing:

Dear Pan,

Thank you for being my friend. And thank you for your advice on the friends I have already. I took your suggestion and have set up to meet with some fellows I have known pretty much all my life. I'm looking forward to that.

Because you are my friend, I wondered if I could share something that has bothered me. I sometimes feel like I am doing some better, but then I keep going to these deep caves of sadness somewhere inside my head and when I am there, at first, I feel like I need to stay there, that somehow staying there and looking at the walls of the caves, in some magical, mystical way it's going to help me feel better, that it's going to help me heal but the simple truth is, it really doesn't. It does not make me feel any better to go into these deep dark holes. It only makes me feel worse. It only sinks me deep down into sorrow and so then I try to not let myself fall into those holes. I can't help it. I still go down the holes, but they don't help. There's nothing about them that helps me. There's nothing they do that helps me heal this deep, unremitting sorrow I feel when I am there. And so I guess it is a balance between allowing myself to grieve and feeling the pain but at the same time knowing that the pain itself doesn't heal a thing. Nothing actually cures my broken heart. I think there is no healing. There's only time, I guess. There's only the opportunity to sometimes think of something else over time, to do other things, and if I have enough other experiences in life, if I actually do other things, then maybe I will have other things to think about, if only for a little while, and that's the only difference that time gives me. It's not that time itself makes my loss less painful, it is that time and just going on with life covers my memories with new experiences, and, hopefully, over time all those new experiences will give me some little bit of respite, some little bit of peace. That is maybe all I can ask for.

This is what I am feeling today. I hope it is okay that I tell you. I needed to tell someone.

Your friend,

Raliv

The little missive had taken up the better part of two pages of Raliv's scratchy writing, but it was legible enough. He tore the pages out and folded them in half and then in half again and put it in his shirt pocket. He picked up the items he had unloaded from his pockets the day before. He dropped his pocketknife into his front pocket, and picked up the recorder from the table, zipping it into his bomber jacket he had pulled from the closet. He looked at the pad of paper again, the numbers folded back and the blank sheet before him. He clicked the pen, leaned over, and wrote the year and then words: "My Trip to."

Then he paused. Where would he go? He put the pen in his pocket with the note and his To Do list and headed towards the door. He stopped before he got there and dribbled some water onto the broccoli seed sets he was starting. He had brought two new pair of tube socks from his room, since he himself always liked getting socks as presents. They were in his other front pocket. He had a whole drawer full of white tube socks. Colleen laughed at his white socks habit, but he insisted that he never had to worry about matching up sock pairs, and they were comfortable. He zipped up his coat and snatched his keys from the key hook, causing the one loose end to pull away from the wall. It was okay. It was on his list. He went outside.

Sunlight streamed across the yard. All the snow was now gone and even the bomber jacket threatened to be too heavy for the day, but maybe that was more from the sunlight than the air temperature. Raliv was heading toward his truck when he remembered another chore for today: "Replace Truck Battery." He would write it down on his list so he could mark it off. Marking the chores off his list gave him a small sense of satisfaction. He headed instead for the SUV, climbed in, and headed towards the meadow.

As Raliv approached the chair, his heartbeat quickened. Returning each day to find a note from Pan had become a highlight to his daily routine. He could see a long stick leaning up against the chair. He stopped the car and stepped towards the chair. It was a long, vine-twisted walking stick, with a whittled-down gripping spot. A loop of rabbit leather was attached to the wood above the grip.

He came to the chair and picked up the cane. He held it to his side, slipped the strap over his hand, and held it to his side. He jabbed the ground with it to feel its heft. It was strong but not heavy. The dimensions were just right. A walking stick. Why didn't he already have one, he wondered. It was something he knew he would use.

Raliv took Pan's note from the crevasse in the wood and wedged the letter he had written into it. He lay the socks on top. Then he sat down to read his message from Pan. It too was several pages of square block letters, although on the smaller sheets of the notepad he had left before.

My friend Raliv,

A woodsman needs a good staff in the forest so he can check for holes and such and to help relieve your back. I made this one for you. I heard you playing yesterday. It was lovely. Isn't it amazing what you find you can do? I was very comfortable on the soft rug, so please do not be concerned about that. Thank you so much for the fruits and vegetables. I love oranges and almost never get to have them. I am very glad your family came. I see you. I see you beginning to get better.

Sometimes folks who don't understand grief may want to know how you are doing and to some extent what they might be asking is along the lines of, "Are you getting over it?" They don't ask it to be mean. It's just because they don't understand what grieving feels like. The truth is it's a bit like when you hurt your back and it hurt too much to move. Slowly, you learned which way you could turn, how far you could reach without pulling yourself down in pain. It's something you will learn over time and by having family and friends come by and by playing music. Each of those things stretches your grieving muscle just a tiny bit. In time, you will be able to bend over, but for now, you have to be satisfied with being able to stand.

In true friendship, Pan

Raliv sat there for several minutes, thinking over Pan's note. It made him feel better. He liked the analogy, understood it, and he took comfort from the fact that his back no longer hurt, so maybe, in time, he would not be so sad, just as Pan said.

He was being watched. He could sense it. Before, he had ignored the feeling of being watched, but today, Raliv wanted to acknowledge it. What might Raliv do to respond to being watched? If Pan were going to see him, perhaps Raliv should do something to let Pan know he was aware of being watched. But what? It wasn't as if Raliv was going to suddenly dance a little jig here in the meadow. Even if he had felt spry enough for that, he didn't feel that happy-go-lucky.

Then he remembered he had his little flute in his pocket and Pan had said they liked his playing. He took it out and played the song he was learning now, the Peruvian one. He got the first part pretty well, but it was slower on the last part that he had practiced less on. He sat on the chair, facing the osprey nest, playing a song for his hidden friend. And playing for the raptors too, he supposed, and the rabbits that first led him to Pan, and to the chorus frogs in the pond behind him. There were deer who bedded down in the Johnson grass and Queen Anne's lace on the other side of the meadow – he played for them too.

When he reached the end of the part of the song he had taught himself, he kept playing, searching for any note that might be the next note. He played for several minutes, then put the recorder back in his pocket and surveyed the field, the edge of the woods, the weedy fencerow that marked the where the pasture ended and another began. Whatever that song had been, he liked it, and he liked that he had made it up himself. It was Raliv's song. He felt a small smile form on his face.

Raliv returned to the car and headed back the house. He was ready to tackle his list.

Chapter 12

The To Do list worked well. Raliv marched through the remainder of the day doing chore after chore. He brought the jumper cables out of the garage and started up the truck using the SUV. Then he drove to the auto parts store and bought a new battery, using various wrenches and screw drivers from a bin of used tools at the shop to pull the old battery and install the new one.

He vacuumed the living room and hall floors, cleaned baths, laundered clothes, fixed loosened screws and generally had a satisfying day of puttering. Getting even small things done felt so rewarding. Crossing each item off was a tiny little victory. He prepared a large casserole, dividing it into individual ramekins and freezing all but the one he was having for dinner so that he could have a meal at the ready for another four nights, although he doubted he would eat them on consecutive evenings. He had, it turned out, a huge supply of ramekins from when he and Colleen had held a dinner party and served French onion soup as a starter. If the night before had been a bad one, this night was much better.

After dinner, Raliv had sat at the kitchen table until late, drawing the design for the piece of furniture for the entry. He used a yellow pencil and a wooden ruler with a metal edge, both left over from his teaching supplies. He drew a front view, then a side view, then a perspective, using dotted lines for the edges that would be hidden from view. Fishing out one of his dozen or more tape measures he had accumulated over the years from a drawer, he measured and remeasured the wall and the floor and drafted out the design carefully, the magazine folded back to the page that showed the piece he was modelling the piece after.

Numbers scrawled along the margin and Raliv had made a preliminary list of the wood he would need: two-by-fours, three-quarter-inch plywood, one-by-four boards, screws to countersink. He had been so delighted to have the plan done, he had put a period on the last length of wood he needed with such emphasis he had broken the point off the pencil. But no worry; he knew what he had to get to start. He didn't want to over purchase either. He would start with the frame, of course, and then the back, which would give it substance and stability. He would cut the boards in his workshop and build it right here in the kitchen so he would not need to try to move it. It would be heavy once built.

Even though it was late when he finished his design, Raliv had sat up afterwards, energized by the string of small victories, sipping a small pour of bourbon and playing his recorder. Felicity slept on his lap while he played, first the songs he knew, then the one he was still learning, and then just a part of the tune he recalled playing for Pan, a simple six tone sequence that trilled up and back in a kind of broken vee of notes, like a flock of geese flying high overhead.

He liked the sound of it and played it repeatedly, varying the notes a little each time. He had slept well and dreamt just before waking that he and Colleen were in her car, Colleen driving. She had gotten impatient with a slower moving vehicle and gone to pass but the SUV went flying off a cliff, only to land on a road beneath. It turned out to be the road she had been looking for, except they were traveling the wrong direction. Raliv had found a place for them to turn around and then they were driving merrily towards whatever destination they had been intending, singing with the car stereo.

It was a good dream, Raliv decided when we woke up. Even

the part about flying off the cliff had not felt afraid. Colleen was driving, so they were fine.

Now he sat at the kitchen table, reviewing his plan. It was so odd, he thought, to have these peaks and valleys in his days, one day so heavy with grief and the next more relaxed, almost able to be himself. He tried to put the idea out of his head. Sipping on a cup of espresso, he eyed the space he was going to put the bench, then the drawing.

He pushed back the plate that had held his English muffin and egg. It would work. The mud-foyer bench would be a great addition, not too large, but adding to the ability to keep things tidy and at the ready at the same time. He thought today he would go get the wood from Fred's store. He needed to copy down the part of his materials list that would suffice for the first stage of building. He retreated to the den to sharpen the pencil. Colleen had a battery-powered pencil sharpener by her desk. Raliv pushed the pencil in and the grinder did its job, but then Raliv saw the paper sleeve of a CD sitting on the shelf next to the computer. His writing was on it: "Our Playlist." He had almost forgotten making this for her.

It was a collection of some of their favorite songs, a mixed set of classics and new pieces, plaintive ballads and love songs and songs they had heard from street musicians on their travels. The Andean group was represented and a guitarist they had enjoyed listening to in Piazza Navona while they drank Aperol spritz's and munched on olives. There was a song by two women from New Orleans, one a guitarist the other a violinist. Raliv had had great fun making the CD for them to listen to as they drove around or as they busied themselves with making dinner.

He looked around to find the CD itself then realized Colleen was probably listening to it on her computer. He turned it on and let it boot up, pressed the button on the CD shelf and out pushed the CD. It also had "Our Playlist" written on it, but in Colleen's writing since Raliv had neglected to do so. He took it out and put it in its sleeve, turned off the computer, and returned to the kitchen.

He just might listen to it, if it wasn't too difficult a memory. But today, he thought it would be okay. He wanted to think about Colleen, wanted to relive the fun, the warmth, the love. He considered playing the disk on the player in the kitchen, a small unit that gave out surprisingly good sound, but decided that it could come later.

He maybe should head to Fred's for wood first. That was all there was on the list for the bench today – "Get wood." He would take his sweet time with this project. It is how he wanted to approach it. He would get the wood and unload it into his workshop and then he could go check the chair and see if there was a message. He felt just a little bad for unloading his heavy sorrow yesterday on Pan and maybe would even apologize, if Pan called him out on it. He would take a pad with him and not write the note ahead of time, just in case. Raliv returned to the kitchen, cleaned up his breakfast, checked the broccoli seeds, and headed out.

The sun was shining, and it finally felt like spring outside. A slight breeze was wagging the leaves of the forsythia bush just ready to explode in yellow by the back door. A black and white warbler gave out its thin, reedy whisper of a song from a low branch on the maple tree. Raliv had his mission and it gave him a spring in his step.

The truck started without a hiccup and Raliv drove into town. The pretty day had brought people out and traffic was busy, although as small as the town was, there was still nothing resembling a traffic jam. At the hardware store, Raliv helped himself to a bag of popcorn. He wasn't at all hungry, but the smell as he opened the door of the shop of the freshly popped corn was too enticing.

He gave his list to the clerk, waved hello to Fred, added a large bag of black sunflower seeds for his feeder to the order, then drove to the back building for it all to be loaded into the truck. Raliv sat in his old truck, munching happily on the salty popcorn, waiting his turn. Colleen would have loved this project. What color would she want it to be? Yellow to match the walls?

Pan and the Message Chair

No, white. A washable semi-gloss white. By the time the two men in the warehouse had loaded the lumber and the birdseed, Raliv had eaten the entire bag of popcorn.

Raliv drove by the burger place for a cup of unsweetened iced tea, then went home. The mail had piled up again, since he kept forgetting to check it, but it was all junk mail, catalogs for Colleen, ads for satellite television, notices of check-cashing places. It would all be good fire starter, Raliv decided.

When he arrived at his workshop, he unloaded all the lumber except the plywood, which was too heavy and unwieldy for him. He had just gotten over a bad back and did not want to wrench it again. He decided the truck bed could be his cutting table for the plywood. And maybe John would have to help him assemble that part. He lay the lumber he could carry on the table in his workshop. He would make his first cuts tomorrow, after checking and rechecking his measurements.

It felt good to just have this little first part done. He had made the commitment to do it now. He had the wood, and it was now in the workshop. He looked it over appreciatively. He had asked for the best pieces they could find, and the men had chosen well. He straightened the boards so they lay flat and saw on the shelf behind them his old radio and CD player.

Raliv blinked. It was electric, but also ran on batteries. That would work out at the cabin, he thought. He had wanted to take a radio out to the cabin, and this was even better. He plugged it in and switched the knob to radio and static came out. He tuned a bit, and a Spanish radio station came on, then twisted some more until a country song came on through the speakers. It worked.

He smiled. He needed batteries. Fortunately, he had a horde of batteries Colleen had gathered in case the power went out in the house. This thing took, what, four C batteries? Raliv had those, he knew. He turned it off, unplugged it, and carried it towards the workshop door.

Before he made the door, he saw a length of thin jute rope hanging from a hook. He picked up the rope for Pan and

145

returned to his truck. He would make a quick detour to the kitchen for batteries and the CD then head out to the chair and then to the cabin to feed the birds. He just might stay there. He could take one of the casseroles with him for dinner, and maybe some ham for breakfast the next day. True, he had just had the same meal last night, but that didn't bother him. It was tasty and, even better, already made.

He took the rope and the radio out to the truck and put them in the back. He would take Felicity too. Her carrier always sat on the bench seat next to him. He wanted her company. He thought maybe he would take some warmer weather clothes out while he was at it. The weather was breaking and Raliv wanted to be ready.

In the kitchen, Raliv put a slice of country ham in a plastic bag and took one of the frozen casseroles and put both into an insulated lunch bag along with a frozen cooler bag. He sorted through the drawer where they kept the batteries and found what he needed for the radio. He put the batteries and the CD in a brown paper shopping bag. He dribbled water on the broccoli seeds, then went to his room, tugged a travel bag down from the closet shelf, and put in some cargo pants, some tee shirts, some underwear, and some white socks.

As he passed through the living room, he slid the recorder into a side pocket of the bag. Felicity slept on Colleen's chair. Raliv tried not to let on he was about to retrieve the carrier for fear she would run and hide, but she never opened her eyes. He picked up the calico who lazed comfortably in his hands and took her to the carrier he had stood on its end. She squirmed a little, pressed her hind foot against the opening, but he had done this enough it went off relatively smoothly. She never wanted to go in, but once in, she was usually calm until they got into the truck. She hated the truck and meowed loudly the entire journey no matter how long a trip it was. He scooped a baggie full of dry food for the cat since a casserole was probably not the best idea for her dinner. He scooped extra just to have some in storage at the cabin.

Pan and the Message Chair

It took two trips to carry everything to the truck, the last one including his new walking stick. He cranked up the truck and Felicity gave out a loud "Meow." The shocks on the old truck were no longer very stiff and the added weight of the plywood still in the back made the truck feel like a boat cutting through choppy water as he drove the familiar route past the barn and the rose of Sharon bushes, across the field, and through the opening in the fallen fence at the catalpa tree.

There was the message chair and there was something on it. Raliv felt a small dread come over him. Had he unloaded too much onto this new friend? Had he assumed too much? He worried he might scare away his friend he had just made. He took his notepad and pen and retrieved the rope from the back of the truck and made his way to the chair.

Resting on the chair were two shed deer antlers, each of them four points and they were nearly identical. The chocolate brown mottling at the thick end gave way to long, white, curled spikes at the end. They were beautiful and Raliv immediately knew how he could use them. They would be perfect for the hooks on the mud-foyer bench. In his plan he had drawn wrought iron hooks to contrast with the white paint he imagined, but these would be even better, and would make the bench into an entirely different level of artistry. Perfect.

Raliv fished the note from the slot in the wood, took a deep breath, and started reading.

My friend Raliv,

I know you hurt in ways you never knew you could, in places you maybe didn't know you had. It is okay to hurt. Trying to control your pain only makes it worse. Only you know how you feel, but however you feel, it cannot be wrong. Let your love for Colleen carry

you forward. Hold her close, and she
will always be with you. Others will
come and go in your life, but you will
always have your love for your wife and
her love for you. And I am always glad
to share your load with you, even if I
am not always here.

I loved your music. You make a fine
flute player. The part you wrote was
the best part. I felt like it was a
composition from your heart and that
made it all the more beautiful.

Your dear friend,

Pan.

Raliv sat now on the chair next to the antlers and gave
out a deep sigh. There was much to unpack from this message.
First, Raliv had not frightened Pan away. He was very glad of
that. Second, Pan had used Colleen's name. Raliv remembered
he had told Pan in one of the notes her name, but this was the
first time Pan had used it. It felt close. It felt natural and familiar
and close, as if Pan were also friends with Colleen now. Raliv
thought maybe so. But it also felt new and different.

And then there was the part about "not always here." Was
that a hint that Pan was getting ready to leave? Pan was a traveler
and Raliv knew that. And it made sense that a traveler travels. If
he could not be angry with Felicity for being a cat, he could not
feel bad if Pan traveled. But it did make him feel just a bit hollow,
knowing he might soon be missing his friend. It felt like another
loss coming, in its way.

But this was different, too. He had only just met Pan.
Rather, he had not yet met Pan. No, it didn't make him happy,

but it would not be the same at all. In some ways, he had always known Pan would leave, hadn't he? The advice Pan had given him was true, Raliv knew. He would always have Colleen's love and his love for her, no matter what might transpire over the coming years. He needed to embrace that. He steadied the pad on his knee and wrote a message to Pan:

My Dear Friend Pan,

Thank you for your encouraging words. They mean a lot to me. I don't know why some days are so hard and others seem to be better. Today is a better day. Sometimes, life confuses me. Sometimes, I wonder why there isn't some answer I can come up with to help me through these days. I am a mathematician. I am used to specific answers. Problems have solutions. Even if a number can't be known in some equation, in my world, it can be approached. I wish I knew how to figure out this calculation. It is hard for me to not know the answer.

I am glad you enjoyed my song. It wasn't a composition, exactly. Just a mish-mash of different songs and some parts I made up as I went along. The truth is, I don't know what songs to play. I love music but I don't know many songs and I don't really know much about music. But I will keep trying because playing does make me feel better. Maybe playing my flute is a part of my equation?

I sense that you are thinking about moving on soon. I won't tell you to stay. I know you have to do what you feel is right for you. But please know that whenever you do, I will miss you. And you are always welcome here.

I brought you some rope. I hope you find it useful. It's not very thick but I figure that will make it lighter to carry. I have always liked having rope around, even as a boy. Some things I guess I just never outgrew.

Your friend,

Raliv

He tore out the two leaves of paper he had written on and folded them into the gap of the chair. Then he took his recorder and played for a few minutes. He had learned more of "El Condor Pasa" and played that first. Then he played the French melody, "Au Clair de la Lune." Then he played the parts he had made up, the six notes, turned this way, then another. He let the notes fall into a set pattern, then faded the volume away. He liked the effect. But he had things he wanted to do, and he had left Felicity in the truck, so he grabbed the antlers and his note and walked back to the truck.

He drove back to the cabin thinking about his little composition. "Raliv's Song" he had named it in his head before, but it was really Pan's song. It was easy enough to play and to have fun with. He could probably teach JJ and Becky and even Joey and Megan to play it, although the younger two would be harder, but they were smart, good kids. They could do it.

Pan and the Message Chair

Wouldn't that be a sight, Raliv teaching his grandchildren to play recorders? Mrs. Wiggington would love it wherever she was. What justice would she feel when the four grandchildren blew as hard as they could to make the whistles shriek, as they would have to? The urge to blast a shriek from the recorder is evidently too overpowering for a child.

Raliv pictured it in his mind's eye. He didn't really want all of them playing his recorder. And he needed to be able to play along with them. But of course, he knew where the bamboo grew. He had a model to use right there on the truck seat next to him. He could make his way to the tailwaters of the beaver pond and cut some bamboo sections and take his time and make little recorders for all four grandchildren. And if he made sure to make them the same length and put everything in the same place as his own, they would all be more or less in tune with each other, which would be far easier to teach on and far more pleasant to listen to.

What was today, Tuesday? JJ and Becky were coming out Saturday. He could surely finish two recorders by then. Maybe even all of them and he could get Brian and Stacey to bring the other kids too. He had that lunch with his old friends, but he would be back by three at the latest. They could all come to Grandad's and eat pizza and drink sodas and learn to play recorders.

He liked the plan. He would call his sons when he returned to the house tomorrow. Or maybe even climb to the top of the hill with the cellphone and send them messages this afternoon. Why not? It was a beautiful day to take his new walking stick and hike up the hillside and make plans with his family. It was a good plan, he decided. All of it. Making recorders, being with family, sharing his new-found music, taking a walk with his staff, all of it felt right today.

He put Felicity in the cabin and set up her area with a litter box, water bowl, and dry food bowl. He put the bag with his own meals in the pantry, just to be sure Felicity did not get adventurous. The casserole was still frozen. It would all be fine.

He took his walking stick and the recorder and climbed the hill first. He sent the message to his sons, inviting them all to come out Saturday, but he didn't wait to hear back. Instead he walked along the hillside then climbed down to the creek bottom below. He took his pocketknife and sawed five sections of bamboo to make the recorders, including an extra piece if he messed one up. Then he followed the creek to the beaver pond.

From the back of the cabin, he and Colleen had watched the seasons pass in the beaver pond. It was coming to life now in the spring, the tree frogs singing already in the warm afternoon. Turtles lined up on logs, sunning. A great blue heron squawked coarsely and flew away as Raliv made his way along the bank. Sunfish swirled the water around their muddy nests, roiling the surface. In summer, the dragonflies would be darting across the water and rails and tanagers would fly in. By autumn, everything would turn yellow-orange and geese would fly in to rest on their way south. Watching and hearing the seasons change on the pond was more reliable than a calendar.

Raliv sat on a fallen log beside the pond and gazed out at the water. He picked up a pebble and tossed it into a deeper part of the pond and it landed with a hollow plop, sending rings of ripples waving across the placid water.

He could feel Colleen with him. They had sat on this very log, daydreaming and watching the life unfold all around them. He knew she was there with him any time he came here. She was there with him in every tree, in every branch. and in every leaf. She watched with him every bird that flew to the feeder by the cabin and back down to the pond. She saw with Raliv every squirrel that hopped around the fallen logs and every little animal in the woods.

This was their world. They built this world together, so if he was in this world, he was with Colleen and she was with him. How could he ever go wrong as long as he had her in this world together? That was what he needed to take from the grace of Colleen's love. He was with her anytime he was in their house, anytime he was in these woods, and anytime he was enjoying this beautiful world that they had built together.

"Thank you," he said aloud. "Thank you for being here with me, Sweetheart." He sat for a long time on the log, watching and remembering.

Chapter 13

Raliv and Felicity enjoyed the night at the cabin. For a while, Raliv worked on the recorders by the woodpile, studying the one Pan had made him carefully. Felicity watched from the window. He had had to knock out center nodes in the bamboo pieces by ramming a metal bar through the middle and tapping it through with the back of his axe. One of the pieces split when he did this, but he had cut an extra piece, so it was fine.

He used a hack saw he had fished out of the shed to even out the cuts and used a rasp that had once been his father's to even out the edges. He measured each piece against Pan's handiwork, marking the spot and shape of each finger hole with a pencil. He would use various sized drill bits to drill them out, although Pan had obviously carved the holes in Raliv's recorder with a knife. But Raliv wasn't confident in his ability to carve out each hole the right size. He would make the holes and sand it smooth back at his workshop, he decided. He needed a short piece of wood, a small section of dowel perhaps, to block one end, and another piece to carve into the mouthpiece, but he had a start. That was plenty for today.

When the sun started setting, it was cool enough for a fire in the fireplace so Raliv and his cat sat by the fire, Raliv just staring absently into the flames, the calico sleeping on Colleen's chair. Raliv daydreamed about what he would plant in Colleen's garden, now his garden.

Colleen loved green beans, yellow squash, and tomatoes. Especially tomatoes. She would walk along the row of tomato plants, find one that was bright crimson, pluck it, wipe it on her shirt, and bite into it right there, eating it as if it were an apple with no core.

There would be those vegetables, of course, but Raliv would add onions to the garden. Colleen did not like onions, although she had learned to cook with them in a manner that she could enjoy the flavor without the texture, which is what she said turned her off. But even then, she didn't put very much onion in anything. But Raliv loved onions and was now eating onions just about daily, a thick slice on a sandwich, several healthy cubes in a plate of beans, or even a half of a small onion cooked atop a pork chop. Onions were definitely going into the garden.

And eggplant. As much as anything, Raliv wanted to watch the shiny purple fruits form day by day in the garden. And he thought he would have one and only one zucchini plant, which would provide him with more squash than he would ever want.

He gazed into the flickering fire, watching in his mind as the rows of green plants sprouted in the garden. Then he got up and found a juice glass that had once been a jelly jar and poured a finger and a half of bourbon into it. He returned to his chair and let himself be warmed by the flames and the whisky and his image of a summer garden. After a few minutes, he played his recorder. He had finished learning the Andean song and was now picking out "Amazing Grace," which was coming faster than "El Condor Pasa," partly because it was an easier melody, but also because Raliv was growing more comfortable with the instrument.

Raliv grew tired of playing and remembered the radio/CD player he had brought from his workshop. He put the batteries in and tried to tune to a radio station, but the valley the cabin sat in kept him from getting much so he plopped in the CD and listened to "Our Soundtrack" while he sipped the last bit of bourbon in his glass. Felicity did not move.

Dan and the Message Chair

Raliv let his memory and the music from the CD take him to all the places he and Colleen had gone. There was a love song popular when they had gone to the beach on their honeymoon. There was the Italian operatic singer they had first heard at a restaurant near Pier Seven in San Francisco. The travel songs mixed with the favorites from their past in a pleasant weave of melodies.

Then, one of their long-time favorite songs came on, a ballad about two people still in love after many years, still enjoying a romantic dance in the moonlight. It was a song from their lives that always included a kitchen dance for Raliv and Colleen, holding each other close, swaying gently around the table and countertops.

Raliv had forgotten it was on the playlist, and when it came on, his first reaction was to not hear it, to turn it off as too difficult to hear, reminding him again of his loss. But their kitchen dances were tender, close moments, and he didn't want to lose that. Raliv looked up at the mantle at the photo of the two of them on the beach at Lover's Key in Florida. He stood, picked up the picture, and danced around the cabin, slowly, gently, staring at the photo, dancing with his sweet wife again. He held her picture, gazing at her beautiful face. It felt so good to have another kitchen dance with her.

Felicity raised her head and watched him step carefully, delicately around the cabin. His eyes watered, but they were bittersweet tears. He was glad to have had the dance with Colleen. He switched off the CD and finished off the last sip of bourbon and went to bed. Felicity jumped up on the bed and slept nestled close to his legs.

Raliv woke up early, the sun streaming through the window, a faint rose beam of light resting on his blanket from the crystal on the sill. Felicity had leapt off the bed sometime in the night. He made his coffee and fried up the ham slice and sat at the picnic table to soak up the brisk, bright sunlight.

The cat yawned behind the screen in the open doorway. The flowers that had been nipped by the cold were already starting to return, their thin spires of leaves a testament of their resilience. A prothonotary warbler flitted in and out of a hole in a topless white oak stob, his golden color flashing in the sunlight. He flew low on the poplar branches beyond the flower bed, stopping every now and again to give out his thin tweet-tweet-tweet-tweet. A chipmunk sniffed his way across the yard. The trees were showing their budding leaves and dancing slightly in the early morning breeze. In another month, where he was sitting would be covered with a dappled light.

The ham was salty and satisfying, but he wished he had had a biscuit or something to round it out. But no matter. Raliv was eager to get to his workshop and start cutting the lumber for the bench by the back door and to work on the recorders. He returned to the cabin, washed up his dishes, loaded Felicity back into her kennel, and got ready to go work on his projects.

In the shed, Raliv had seen a small green tarp that he had used to cover the woodpile last summer. It was only four-by-six so not really large enough for the job, but it had been a promotional item at Fred's store, so Raliv had picked it up. Ropes and tarps were his weakness. If Colleen was forever buying new dishes, at least they could eat off of them. Raliv simply kept his treasures in case he needed them, which it seemed he rarely did. He retrieved the tarp and put it in the back of the truck.

Felicity sat in her kennel on the seat next to him, gazing out nonchalantly. Raliv started up the truck and she started her meowing. By the time they reached the message chair, her meowing was insistent, but as soon as he turned off the truck, she stopped. The morning was warming up, so he rolled down the window of the cab to keep his cat from getting too warm. Raliv took his recorder and the pad and pen, then pulled the neatly folded tarp from the back of the truck, and walked towards the chair.

There was something on it already. Raliv was glad for that. He came to the chair and found a small stack of flat rope pieces. It was a pair of intricate Turk's head knots, woven into flat little pads. Pan had turned sections of the rope he received only yesterday into beautiful knots. But what were they for?

Raliv picked them up and inspected them. He had seen knots like these in gift shops. They were coasters, he realized. It was true, he had no coasters in the cabin. The furniture in the cabin was pretty battered and abused when they put it in, and they rarely had ice in their drinks so condensation really wasn't an issue, but Colleen had said something about needing some, if for no other reason than they would make the cabin look homier. These would be perfect. How had Pan made these overnight, he wondered. He slid Pan's note from the gash in the seat of the chair.

My dear friend,

I understand your frustration about life and what it all means. Here is what I have found about life during my travels. Life is a puzzle. You wake up every day and try to work your way through today's puzzle. I don't think there is an answer, no one answer. There is only the getting out of bed and living each day according to what it brings. We may make goals and plan for the future, but in the end, we only live in the present, and the present is no more than a riddle to be unraveled according to the clues we are given. Looking for a single solution would mean life is a problem, but it is only a problem if there are unknowns. You know all there is to know about your world. Take strength from that. And try to forgive yourself for your doubts. I think they are normal.

You say you don't really know about music, but you are surrounded by music. You have the music of birds and frogs and the forest and even the grasses. You don't have to play those songs. Just play your accompaniment to those songs, as you did that day here at the chair. That is beautiful music. And yes, I think music is very much a part of figuring things out in our hearts.

You mentioned my leaving. It is true I am getting ready to move on soon. I get restless if I stay too long and I never want to overstay my welcome. But I will not leave without saying goodbye.

Your friend,

Pan

Raliv sat on the chair and reread the note. Was Pan right? Was there no one answer, only living out each day? Raliv loved planning, but even planning was a way of living in a moment. He loved making plans. He and Colleen planned trips and gardens and menus. They made Christmas lists in June and started jotting down ideas and marking the names with checks when the presents were gathered. But the list itself was a part of the way they celebrated the holidays, along with watching every Christmas movie over and over. They knew all the lines of the classics and Raliv even got a knot in his throat at the same place in the film each year when Scrooge finally asks his nephew's wife to forgive him.

It was odd that his thoughts had turned to Christmas. It was just beginning to feel like spring and the holidays were a long way off. They had not been able to celebrate the season much this past year. Colleen had been very sick and Raliv had not left her side so there simply was neither time nor energy for it.

She had not asked for much from Raliv regarding the future once she knew she would not recover, but she did ask that he not start hating Christmas because of her illness, that he continue to enjoy it the way they always had. He had agreed to do his best. In her way, she was telling him to live in the present as well, he realized. He should not be mired in his memories of happier times, and especially of difficult times.

Pan was right too. Each day was a riddle, a small mystery that he had all the clues to figuring out. He only had to piece it together each day. And sometimes that mystery involved lists, but that was a portion of it. That was solving the puzzle.

Then Raliv reread the part about forgiving himself. That one line resonated with him. He had often felt guilty whenever he thought about Colleen's illness. If only he had gotten her to the doctor sooner or if he had been able to help her more in some way, he found himself troubling over, then perhaps it could have been different, maybe she would still be here.

But he knew, deep down, that there was nothing anyone could do. They had tried to beat the cancer, but it simply was not possible. And then, lately, when he found himself feeling a little stronger and not as sad, he had felt guilty for feeling better, as if he were betraying his Colleen by healing. He knew it was nonsense, of course. If anyone in the universe would want Raliv to get better and to find some way to move ahead, it would be Colleen. Raliv took the pad of paper and wrote his note.

My good friend Pan,

Thank you for the coasters. They are truly surprising and beautiful. You have so many talents. I am working on making some recorders for my grandchildren. I want to teach them to play, if I can.

I appreciate your wisdom more than you know. It helps me tremendously. You know, sometimes I feel like the luckiest man in the world to have found and won her love, to have become that unit that was us, and at the same time, the unluckiest man ever to have lost that true and precious love. But I think I will choose to take the lucky part as my guiding light and try to live in the present as much as I can.

And I want to say, I forgive myself.

Raliv paused and reread his last sentence. His throat tightened, and then he continued.

That feels so strange to write that line. I never knew how hard that would be to write and to think about. I am going to go and work on a piece of furniture I have designed. I want to enjoy myself and choose to feel lucky to have loved Colleen. Thank you for that precious gift. So often, I worry about what to do next with my life.

Here is a tarp I had. I hope it will provide you with some shelter as you make your way wherever you go. I do not look forward to your leaving, but I do want you to be safe on your travels. I hope you know that you will always be welcome to return. I hope you do. I want you to know I look forward to our letters. They are an important part of my day. I will miss them.

Your friend,

Raliv

He folded up the message and slid it into the slot in the chair. He lifted the recorder to his mouth and played Pan's Song again, although of course it was different this time. He added notes to the trill, worked in a sequence from "Amazing Grace," returned to the plaintive sound of "Au Clair de la Lune." The song lifted on the sunlight and fell down through the meadow and across to the tree line.

One of the ospreys circled above, whistling. A downy woodpecker at the edge of the woods gave a rapid drumming. A bull frog gave an occasional grunt from the edge of the pond. The breeze rustled the wild carrot and Johnson grass and the red oak tree let out a squeak as two limbs rubbed together. Raliv didn't play long, but he enjoyed what he had added, or at least most of it. He made a mental note to remember what he had done so he could build upon it. He sat a few minutes longer, thinking about the final part of Pan's message.

Pan was leaving. Raliv had sensed it, had understood it, and had even come to terms with it, but this made it very immediate feeling. Raliv did not like the thought of losing his friend, but then, he wasn't losing them. They were simply going to be someplace else, like his old friends he was meeting on Saturday. Surely, Pan would return if they valued the friendship that had developed over the past, how many days? A week and a half, maybe.

Raliv allowed himself to marvel a little at how quickly he and Pan had become friends, how quickly Raliv had started caring and worrying about this other person. In its own way, that was no doubt a part of the help Pan had been, being someone Raliv could focus on instead of his grief. Did Pan plan for that? But that didn't make sense. Raliv had only stumbled across Pan by accident by coming across a snare set in the forest. No one could have planned something so random, although Pan seemed to know just about everything about the woods, evidently.

Raliv shook the thought from his head. Pan promised to say goodbye, so perhaps that meant Raliv would finally actually see Pan, have a face to put with the advice, the gifts, the caring. That thought sounded promising. He returned to the truck and climbed in. Felicity blinked at him.

"What do you think, Felicity? You like my tune?" He put his fingers through the metal gate to touch Felicity's nose. She sniffed his finger casually, then closed her eyes. "I call it "Pan's Song." He smiled at the calico in the carrier, although she wasn't looking at him. "Maybe my next song will be "Felicity's Follies.""

His heart felt a bit lighter than it had felt in a long time. Raliv started up the truck and the cat opened her eyes and started meowing repeatedly.

Chapter 14

Raliv spent the better part of Wednesday afternoon in his workshop. He had measured again the lengths of wood he needed for the frame of the mud-foyer bench and carefully cut the lumber. He sanded and re-sanded with finer and finer paper until the wood was smooth to the touch. Then he drilled the starter holes for the screws and carried it all inside in several loads.

Once he had all the wood inside, he positioned everything in a mock-up of the frame. This would work. He was pleased with how it was beginning to look. He leaned the wood as close to being assembled as he could then held up the antlers Pan had given him to see how they would look. They measured right but it was hard to see the finished look with only the frame. But that wouldn't be too long now once he cut the plywood and got John and Brian to help.

He retreated to the workshop, put a new blade on his circular saw, and cut the carefully drawn lines on the plywood, pushing it around in the back of the truck to use the bed as his cutting table. There was one cut he could not make, the board being too large and heavy for Raliv to maneuver to that angle, but Raliv was happy with his progress.

John was coming Friday evening and he could help Raliv make the last cut and maybe even help with the sanding. Raliv pushed the mostly cut boards back under the camper top to protect them from the elements and maybe keep the dew out, although if it rained, the top had several holes in it now. But rain hadn't been forecast so he wasn't worried. He headed for the back door.

Raliv hadn't told John about the bench he was making yet. He wanted it to be a surprise. And although John was not at all a handyman around the house, Raliv knew he would be glad to help. Raliv was proud of the man John had become, so attentive to Tina and the kids, but also to Raliv himself. Raliv could not imagine what he might have done the weeks after Colleen's death if John had not been there to support him. It wasn't that John was always at the farm, but he was always available. Raliv knew he could call any time, and often did.

Raliv walked into the kitchen and looked at the lumber, still leaning against the wall in a rough shape of what it would be. He looked forward to John helping him with that last cut and, when Brian and his family came on Saturday, the three of them could put all the pieces together, his sons holding the heavy board while Raliv screwed them into the beginnings of the unit. Once they did that, it would be easy to envision the finished piece. He was tempted to screw together the pieces already in the kitchen, but the large piece was integral to the assembly. *Just be patient*, Raliv reminded himself.

Raliv sat at the kitchen table with a big glass of water. He had broken into a pretty good sweat with the work, but it felt good. It was the sweat of a good afternoon of work. Raliv drank water in big gulps and returned to his thoughts. He wanted to tell John about Pan when he came by himself. He would tell Brian too, of course, but John was the one who lived nearby. He was the one who might be worried more, who would have more questions.

But what would Raliv tell him about Pan? What could he tell John about Pan? Would he simply say he had a friend whom he had never met? That sounded so strange. What was the nature of their friendship, he imagined John asking. Was Pan tall? Short? Raliv didn't even know if Pan was a man or a woman. Maybe the name Pan wasn't even that far off, for all Raliv knew.

He sat at the table and gave out a slight chuckle. Maybe he had made friends with some sort of woodland nymph. He took a long drink and smiled at the absurdity of the thought. No, if it really was a Pan, Raliv would have seen the hoof marks. He grinned at his joke.

The funny thing was, it would not matter to Raliv either way. Whoever they were, they had helped him in a way Raliv could not describe. They had been as true a friend, even in their very short time, as he could imagine. The only other friend he had ever had who was closer was Colleen, and no one would ever know Raliv as well as she did. But Pan gave him thoughtful advice and reassurance without being cloying.

And Pan gave Raliv simple, wonderful gifts, many of them made just for Raliv. They weren't fancy presents and were not what you might find in a store, but the genuineness of thought was so much more valuable than anything money could buy. Raliv had given practical gifts, but he decided that was being thoughtful as well. A traveler would not need trinkets or extravagant gifts. And obviously Pan could make the things they might actually need on the road. So Raliv had given them the kind of things they might find useful.

But he had not given of himself the way Pan had, he realized. Where was Raliv in these presents? He did not feel bad about what he had given Pan, but if Pan was leaving soon, Raliv wanted to give something that maybe would remind Pan of their friendship somewhere down the road, something that maybe would encourage them to return. But what was there to give? He couldn't give Pan a piece of furniture he had made. What would they do with it?

The house telephone rang and Raliv jumped. It was amazing how rarely it rang, and when it did, it seemed to always be a solicitation of some sort. Raliv was tempted to ignore it but went over to check the caller ID. It was the Phelps's number. He picked up the receiver.

"Hello?" Raliv found it odd that people still answered

phones as if it were a question when every caller's identity was generally known.

"Hello, Raliv." It was Mrs. Phelps. Perhaps it was true he had not known which of the two it had been. "I wanted to see how you are doing. How are you?"

"Hi, Mrs. Phelps. I'm . . ."

"Oh please, Raliv. We've been neighbors for twenty years. Call me Barbara."

Raliv leaned against the counter. "Oh, okay, Barbara." Why did it feel so odd the first time to say someone's first name? "I'm doing alright, I think."

"Good."

"It's a process, you know. But I think I'm starting to get my footing some. Everyone else I have spoken with about this who's been through it says it takes time."

"Yes, so I've heard too."

Raliv fiddled with the base of the phone and saw the piece of paper with the pewee drawing on it and slid it out from under the phone. He gave himself a smile and nodded. Perfect. "I will always miss her, Barbara." Raliv returned to the conversation.

"I know, Raliv. I know." Raliv pictured Mrs. Phelps, Barbara now, on the other end of the line. She too was retired from her profession as a pharmacist. In their all-too-rare interactions, he had always liked her, but somehow, between being always preoccupied with his own and Colleen's world and the fact that Barbara was always on the go as well, they had never spoken that much other than greetings passing on the road or brief conversations in stores. "But you wouldn't have it any other way, would you? Missing her means you still love her, right?"

"Yes, that's true." There was a pause.

"Listen, Raliv, Joe and I want to try out that new catfish place in town on Sunday. We wondered if you wanted to come along. I hear they have fabulous frog legs." She said the last part to be enticing.

"You know, I think that sounds great." If he could make fast friends with Pan in ten days, he could make friends with his neighbors after twenty years. "I can't remember the last time I had frog legs. I love them. Should I meet you there?" Raliv looked over the drawing again. He saw a line that was maybe a little thick on one side. But it didn't matter. It was good and it was his own work and he liked it.

"Well, let's go early. They get very busy around noon." Barbara's voice sounded satisfied she had gotten Raliv to agree to go out, not that he had taken much convincing. "Say, eleven-thirty?"

"I'll see you there, Barbara." Raliv hung up the phone and stood the pewee picture on the countertop so he could see it. He had wanted to show it to John, but never mind. He was giving it to Pan today.

Raliv refilled his water glass and turned over the plastic bag with the hamburger patty he had taken out of the freezer earlier to help it thaw more rapidly. Felicity sashayed into the kitchen and gave Raliv a blink. Then she fell onto her side and stretched out her paws. Raliv went over and gave her a pet. The cat rolled over to get petted on the other side. Raliv complied, then stood. "That's enough for now, Felicity. I still have some work to do."

Raliv thought about how infrequently he spoke these days. He liked that he had phone calls and now some lunches set up to have conversations. He liked the cat, but talking with her was just not the same. Well, not talking with, talking to, he supposed. "I'm going back to the workshop." He motioned with his arm and then grinned at himself, telling the cat where he was going.

Out in the workshop, Raliv drilled the various holes in the four recorders. He cut the dowel for the mouthpiece and carved the notch in it like the one Pan had made for him. He sanded everything and was ready for the final assembly, but he decided to wait on that until tomorrow. He had done plenty for one day.

He returned to the kitchen and finished his glass of water. He turned on the radio by the window and the public radio station Colleen often listened to came on with a program of classic jazz. That will do nicely, Raliv decided. He needed some sound in the house. He showered and came back into the kitchen. "Take

Five" was playing on the radio.

Raliv baked a potato to have with his burger. While the potato was cooking, he decided he needed something green, so he put several sprigs of broccoli in a steamer. After he set the meal on the table, he opened a beer and poured it into a glass. He didn't drink beer much, but tonight, it sounded good. "In a Mellow Tone" started on the radio.

The meal looked enticing as he sat at the table. He had added cheese and a big slice of onion to the patty. He sat at the table and looked up at where Colleen would have sat. He felt a familiar emptiness. "I miss you, honey." He set his mouth in a thin line and pictured his wife, sitting at the other end of the table, smiling. He raised his glass in a toast. "To you and me forever, sweetheart."

He took a long gulp of the cool, bitter beer. Always, there was that balancing act, between going back and going forward, between fullness and emptiness, between feeling better and still feeling sad. But he took some comfort in the fact that now, there was at least the semblance of balance. Wasn't that progress?

The beer tasted good. Raliv ate slowly, listening to the music and enjoying the beer. This was his world now. He was moving forward, he felt, but there would be lots of days and evenings like this. It was just the way things were now.

But just maybe he could do this after all.

After he had cleaned up from dinner, he sat in the living room, playing his recorder for a while, then watching a documentary on television about the American Civil War, which he found fascinating. He went to bed late after the documentary, but he slept well. He had gone to bed with his usual "Good night, Sweetheart" wish, but also with an added, "I love it when you come to me in my dreams. Please visit me tonight, honey." Then he had dreamed about Colleen all night, from a dream about shopping in a large store in New York that he only knew because in his dream he knew, not from any actual recognition, to a dream where he caressed her hip and her waist over and over, repeating, "My beautiful wife. My beautiful wife."

Pan and the Message Chair

Had his invitation opened up his unconscious to the dreams? Had her love that had been so palpable for all those years somehow listened? Or maybe it was even the dreamcatcher. Perhaps it was all of it. Raliv didn't know but his dreams left him feeling full and calm in the morning.

Raliv made his espresso and decided to make crepes for breakfast on Thursday. He had always enjoyed making them for Colleen and for the boys when they were little. He would have to admit, he liked that it came across as a fancy dish even though crepes simply were not that difficult to make. Today he made himself three large crepes and filled them with cream cheese and spooned cherry preserves over them. It was a sweeter meal than he usually ate, but the coffee cut through the sugar nicely.

He had work to do on the grandchildren's recorders, so he was eager to get to the workshop. He wanted also to go get the lumber he needed for the next part of the bench he was working on so that it would be at the ready when he had the time, which he mentally mapped out to be Sunday afternoon when he came back from lunch with Barbara and Joe.

With Saturday full already and Friday filling up, Sunday was the next time he would be able to work on it. But Raliv also did not want it to become like an assignment in his mind. He wanted to be sure he took his time and he wanted to just enjoy doing it, enjoy the various actions of doing it, and then enjoy the finished piece.

Of course, he also wanted to go by the chair. He wanted to give Pan the drawing, something that Raliv had made that Pan could keep and be reminded of their friendship. Maybe if there was something there in Pan's possessions that told them there was a place to go that was welcoming and safe, they would return.

After cleaning up the kitchen from breakfast, Raliv took the pewee sketch out on the porch and sprayed it with a clear varnish Colleen kept for her crafts she did with acrylic paints. Raliv didn't want the drawing to smudge. He left the drawing to dry and stepped out into the yard.

It was spring now. How different the weather had gotten over the course of the week and a half when he had first met Pan. Well, he had not met Pan, really. He had started writing with Pan. Before, it had seemed to rain incessantly. Now, the sun was shining, and a very gentle breeze was making the batch of leaves that had sprung forth on the maple lean back so that the sun caught their undersides. The result was a mottled light across the yard. The grass had sprung up and would need cutting before long.

A ring-necked snake zigged across the fieldstone walk. Raliv watched the snake make its way into the taller grass. Colleen's mother had been deathly afraid of any snake, but Colleen had learned the different snakes, especially the ones that "earned their keep," as she put it. The ring-necked snake was one of the welcome ones.

Up in the hickory tree around the side of the house, a tufted titmouse chirruped out its song. Raliv went back inside for his keys. He jotted down the list for the second lumber load onto another piece of paper and came back out. He pulled out the smaller boards from the plywood cuts and stacked them on the porch. The big piece he left. He would just haul it there and back again rather than hurt his back again.

Driving to town, he headed to Fred's Hardware for the lumber, but he could not stop thinking about his dreams of Colleen the night before. He loved the thought of her visits, even if only in his subconscious, but then a part of him worried that by welcoming his Colleen into his dreams, he was holding on to the past too much. Perhaps. Or perhaps not. It was a conflict within him he supposed was as old as human reflection.

His head knew that this was the world he was in now. Intellectually, he understood that this was the life that he needed to live, and he knew he had no choice but to move from here, from this moment and these circumstances. This was the reality of his life. He had to make his choices based upon what actually was, but his heart could not help but yearn for what had been. His heart would probably always ache for the love, the joy, the incredible one-ness of his and Colleen's life. How could it not?

And that was the conflict he suspected would always be there as it was for the very many who had gone down this path before him and would follow. It was the conflict between the two most human of his traits: his ability to reason and his ability to love.

Raliv got the wood and sorted through the paint samples, looking at the myriad shades of white available. It was surprising just how many choices he had. He picked four shades that he thought looked close to what he had in mind and put them in his shirt pocket to hold up against the yellow paint of the kitchen walls.

Then he swung by the liquor store and picked up a bottle of cabernet sauvignon, his and Colleen's favorite. Raliv had a full weekend coming and decided he wanted to spend tonight at the cabin, just him and not even the cat. But he wanted it to feel a little different too, so he wanted to have some wine, the kind the two of them would have enjoyed, and not the bourbon that Colleen would not have really enjoyed that much. She would occasionally have a small glass at the end of the day, but only very occasionally.

No, tonight, he was having wine at the cabin and listening to the CD he had made and maybe making a fire in the fireplace. He also wanted to take something to fix for supper that would be better than beans or canned fish and he didn't really have the time to hunt today. In fact, when he thought about it, hunting appealed less to him these days. It was incongruous to mourn the passing of a life and then to go out and take a life. It didn't make sense to Raliv. He didn't doubt he might return to it one day, but not yet.

He stopped by the Piggly Wiggly and picked up two chicken thighs, a bag of salad, and a box of macaroni and cheese. He would grill the chicken outside on the kettle grill by the picnic table and the mac and cheese required nothing more than boiling water and emptying a cheese sauce into the cooked pasta. It would not be hard, but it would be tasty, he decided.

As he walked the aisles of the grocery, he picked out a bottled barbeque sauce and a vinaigrette. And he decided to get that bag of barbequed potato chips on the rack by the cash register to snack on, and the candy bar by the conveyer belt. It was Colleen's favorite. He was set.

He checked out and the cashier, whom Raliv recognized as someone that Colleen always engaged in a conversation about the cashier's mother, only smiled and asked him how he was doing, asked him if he collected the stamps, which he did, and wished him a good afternoon.

Back at his farmhouse, Raliv packed an insulated bag with the perishables and added a frozen plastic bottle of water to keep it cold and, later, to just drink as it thawed. He made sure Felicity had what she needed, then he climbed into the SUV to head to the chair and then the cabin.

He left the lumber in the truck. He could get that tomorrow. He had carried out his recorder and Colleen's legal pad and a pen to stop and write his note to Pan. At the last second, he remembered the drawing and picked it up and slid it into a plastic baggie.

The car still needed washing. He would do that tomorrow so it would be clean to take when he drove to see his old friends. He loved his trusted pick-up truck, but he certainly had to admit, Colleen had chosen well with the SUV. It was far more comfortable, especially on a trip that took more than an hour and a half each way. Raliv was excited about seeing his old pals.

Raliv drove past the barn and the unruly fencerow, past the catalpa tree and into the meadow where the chair stood. The sun was shining brightly in a cloudless sky. The little holly tree next to the chair with its deep green leaves shimmered in a small wind. The daffodils were now in full bloom and nodded their yellow heads at Raliv as he drove up, parking the SUV in the middle of the dirt road that led on up through the woods towards the cabin.

An osprey whistled far above him as he exited the car. Behind him, deep in the woods, crows cawed. A bullfrog croaked from the edge of the pond. Raliv could see where deer had bedded down in the Johnson grass just there on the other side of the water. He carried his pad and the drawing over to the chair along with his recorder.

On the chair was the mesh bag he had brought the fruits and vegetables to Pan in. It was filled with pinecones and dried flowers and tied together with a strip of the string. Raliv picked it up and held it to his nose. It was a sachet, and Raliv recognized the scents of lavender and maybe a little bit of rose. Was that yarrow mixed in with it? It was a fresh, clean, floral smell. He inspected it for several minutes, sniffing it and holding it.

Sometimes, the cabin could get a bit stuffy, especially if he had not been there in a while. This would be a great addition and he was on his way there now. That way, every time Raliv came into the cabin, he would have a reminder of his friendship with Pan, at least for a while until the odors faded.

But then he could always add more flowers to it. Maybe he should grow some lavender in the garden. And maybe some sweet alyssum. Yes, why not? Raliv decided he would add flowers to his vegetable garden. And he knew where some lily of the valley grew along a wooded hillside near the creek. He liked the entire idea. Putting the sachet down, he picked up the several pages of folded message that was sitting atop the seat of the chair, weighted down with a small pebble. He sat and read his note.

To my friend Raliv,

Thank you for the tarp. It will come in very handy. You are a good and generous friend.

I will cherish our friendship wherever I go.

Raliv looked up. He recognized where this was going. He

returned to the note.

I am leaving tomorrow at midday. I have one more gift for you I have been working on. I hope you will like it. I won't be able to check the chair tomorrow to receive your present, so please know that I appreciate you. It is an amazing thing to watch you going through this terrible experience in real time. I see you standing now, looking ahead, finding the path that only you can see. You honor Colleen in the way that you live. Another friend once told me, as long as you still say her name, she still lives. So I think it is right to call her name, to see her next to you. All of us must navigate that delicate balance between holding on and letting go. It cannot be wrong to hold onto sorrow as long as you need to. Just be sure to leave some room for other things as well. Maybe think of it as if the grief is a river within you, carving out a canyon that you can fill with happiness one day, all the more so because you have more to fill. I will see you when you are here tomorrow, but I will be making my way along the tree line and then following the stream. As a gift to me, please play for me a song on your flute, and if you play towards the valley, maybe you will hear me playing along with you. Play from your heart and I know it will be beautiful.

Thank you, Raliv, for being such a good friend. I will come back. Listen for me whenever you play to the valley.

Until tomorrow.

Pan

Raliv sat there, rereading the note. He of course knew this was coming, but it still made him sad. His throat tightened. But it was also bittersweet because Pan would return. Raliv had no doubt about that. And when they did, they would be welcome. But this message Raliv was about to write was going to be the last note Pan would receive at least for a time. There was much that Raliv wanted to say before Pan was gone. He took the legal pad and started writing.

My dear friend,

Thank you for the sachet. I know exactly where I want to put it. I will enjoy being

reminded of our friendship each time I smell it.

I won't say that I am not sorry for you to be leaving. I am always sad when I say goodbye to good friends. But I do believe you when you say you will return. I have grown so much since we've become friends. One thing I have come to realize now is that everything doesn't have to mean something, that if I do something it really doesn't has to have meaning beyond my just doing it. I think going forward, I need to just do the things I like to do. They don't have to take on some sense of importance. I don't need to try to make a mark with the rest of my life. I've made my mark. Colleen is my mark. My sons are my mark. My students were my mark. Now I just need to live each day without worrying so much about anything that happens. I think it's a kind of hubris thinking that something I am doing has to have meaning it, has to be important. Everyone I meet, in our own ways, just like you, we're all just living out our days. So I will play my music, but the music is not going to change anything. The noise and the silence of the world are more powerful than my music. I will write to my friends, like you, when I can, but in the bigger picture, writing is not going to change anything. Those who do not read have as much or more power than those who do. I am giving you today a drawing I did. But my art doesn't mean anything. It is only a capturing of a moment of light and there is as much darkness as there is light. As I move forward, I want to be motivated not by a question of "Is it important?" It is only a question of "Is it something I want to do?" Sometimes, I feel like Colleen and I wasted time that I wish we had just enjoyed doing whatever we felt like doing. Maybe that is all any of it really means.

I will certainly grant your request for a song. I will play a song for you today and tomorrow and any time I can make it here to our chair. I have one last request from me: If you do not want me to see you before you go, I will understand. But I would truly love to know what my dear friend looks like. But that is strictly up to you, and I will not hold it against you if you decline. But I am curious.

Forever your friend,

Raliv

Raliv thought maybe he read in the passage telling Raliv just where Pan would be the next day there was a hint that that was where Raliv should look, a sort of invitation. He folded the letter and put it and the drawing under the pebble.

Somewhere in the woods around him, Pan was watching. Raliv knew it. He could feel it. He turned in the chair, took up his recorder and played Pan's Song towards the woods, to wherever Pan might be standing, right now, listening. Of course, once again the melody was different, as it would always be. That was the nature of the song.

As he played, he watched the trees fluttering and saw a spotted fawn and its doe step out along the old powerline track. The Queen Anne's Lace in the field bobbed their dried heads and Raliv let their rhythm become a kind of visual metronome. He could not see Pan, but he decided that was okay. Maybe tomorrow.

He played through the song twice, then faded the volume away. He sat there in the sun for a long time. The doe and fawn grazed at the edge of the woods then disappeared into the trees. He could see an osprey sitting in the big nest, watching.

Raliv returned to the car and drove back to the cabin. He unpacked his foods and busied himself with some light cleaning, but the truth was, he didn't make much of a mess. With it just being Raliv and the cat, with his penchant for cleaning up after himself, things just didn't seem dirty. But he dusted the few pieces of furniture and swept the wooden floor anyway, just to keep it nice. He put the sachet on the mantle near the photo of him and Colleen at the beach. The scent was subtle. He liked it.

Raliv fixed his meal and, sitting at the picnic table, ate as much of it as he could since he really had no way to keep leftovers, although he did decide to keep the rest of the salad. That would be fine. Raliv felt very full. He couldn't remember having such a big meal in a long time.

He cleaned up and as the day began to wane, Raliv took one of the dining table chairs and sat it near the picnic table so he could raise his feet to the bench and use the tabletop for his juice glass of wine. He sat there and looked around him.

The late afternoon sun painted the large branches grey-gold, a sharp contrast to the robin egg blue welkin beyond. A phoebe came and hopped around his chair as he sat, looking at Raliv quizzically but unfrightened and then left in a flutter of flapping feathers to find the feeder. Pink blossom buds filled the ends of the branches on the yellow poplars, bulging, ready to burst. A prothonotary warbler sang out a territorial song in the underbrush. The sunlight so warm and welcome on his skin lulled him to stay longer, doing nothing, doing what he needed most: healing, even if only a little.

And he could feel it.

He missed Colleen constantly, that wouldn't change, but being able to just do nothing, without filling up the day with trivial tasks was already a change. And he could think of her tenderly and lovingly and not burst into tears. That too was a change. Not that he didn't still sometimes cry. He did. But he also no longer tried to hold back the tears. Letting himself cry also felt like healing.

A goose honked down below on the beaver pond, just beyond his sight. A chickadee called out a me-me-me. He realized that was part of what made the anger commingle with the sadness, that he couldn't control it. It wasn't until he didn't try to control it that he could be sad and only sad, and to know it was okay to be sad. It was to be expected, of course.

When he saw it in retrospective, it made sense. Trying to control his grief had only made it more intense.

He took a drink of the wine. It was tart and full and satisfying. He sat there drinking his wine, watching the trees and the flowers and the birds of their world. He heard a great barred owl call from somewhere near the beaver pond and another owl respond from the opposite direction, farther up in the woods. He soaked it all in until the gloaming, then took the chair back inside and sat at his overstuffed chair, listening to Our Soundtrack and enjoying a second glass of wine by the gentle light of the oil lamp.

Chapter 15
Pan

Pan had seen the saplings growing along the back of the fencerow. They were ironwood trees, entwined with honeysuckle. He walked over early, the snow almost completely gone but the ground soggy still. His shoes sank into the boggy ground. His feet were wet.

A bobwhite quail called out with his two-note whistle from deep in the honeysuckle vine. Pan cut a sapling from the bottom and carried it back to his camp. He thought maybe Raliv was finding some footing, and a walking stick was perhaps the right gift, both literally and figuratively. At his camp, he peeled off the vine and bark and measured the height of the cane by standing with the staff up to his body. It was too tall just now for the old man. It was nearly to Pan's shoulder and Pan was a good six inches taller than Raliv.

He took pieces off the bottom of the stick with serrated back of his knife until it was several inches below his own chest. That should be about right. He saved the pieces he cut off for the other whittling project he had in mind. Then he carved out the handle and attached a strip of rabbit leather from the rabbit he had caught that first day he had seen Raliv stumbling along the hillside. That should do. He struck the ground several times to test the strength. Not bad, he decided, and as it aged, it would get even lighter but stay strong.

Pan hoped Raliv was better. He seemed to be, but Pan knew from experience that grief doesn't follow a neat path. He wanted to tell Raliv not to worry about setbacks, about the back and forth that he himself went through, that he supposed most people go through. The walking stick was practical, but it was also a symbol of how Raliv needed to find a way to stand, even if it meant relying on help.

Pan liked hearing the tune the old man played in the woods. That was a good sign, he decided. If Raliv could find a voice for his sorrow through music, that would help him. Then Pan recalled how some folks had mistaken his own grief as a kind of illness that people contract when a loved one passes. It wasn't that they thought it trivial; it was just that it would have been nice to believe that grief was something that could be conquered with medicine or bedrest. He wrote a note to Raliv to tell him that people don't mean harm, and to reassure him that he would find his way, over time. He also wanted to praise his flute playing. It really was remarkable how quickly the old man had taken to the instrument.

Pan leaned the walking stick on the chair and wedged the note into the little notch and stood amid the poplar trees. He whittled on one of the small chunks of wood he had cut from the ironwood stick and waited, glancing up towards the opening in the ruined fence occasionally. When he saw the SUV coming, he stopped carving and stood very still.

The motor of the car had an even purr. He wanted to memorize that sound. He watched Raliv climb out of the car and practically race over to the chair. He had, no doubt, seen the gift from the car. Pan watched as Raliv jabbed at the ground and smiled.

Then the old man sat and read the note. He looked up, at nothing, then read the note again. Pan hoped the message meant what he wanted it to mean. He watched Raliv take a folded note from his shirt pocket and place it in the crevice of wood and lay something white atop it. Did Raliv know Pan was watching, that he always watched?

Raliv turned in the chair and pulled out the recorder from his pocket and began playing. He was playing to the raptors and the quail and the rabbits, but he knew Raliv was playing for Pan too. Pan listened to the tune, the same tune as yesterday until it was different. Now it was something free-flowing and melodic and untethered all at once. The old man was a natural. Unfettered by rules, he was making up his own song. Pan felt a knot form in his throat as he listened.

Then Raliv stood, and using the stick, made his way back to his car. He walked like a man who felt his back was hurting a bit less, who was finding a new way to stretch.

When Pan heard the car's purring sound retreat all the way to the farmhouse, he stepped out of the stand of trees and across to the chair. There were two new pair of thick, perfect socks on the chair. Pan looked down at his mud-covered boots and thought about taking them off right then and putting on the dry, wonderful socks, but decided he really wanted to dry his boots out first. If he put his wet boots on over the socks, he would still have wet feet. But he was certainly looking forward to it.

Then he pulled out the long note from Raliv. It was all about how Raliv felt the grief. It was familiar territory for Pan, and he was glad Raliv wrote to him about it. The man needed a release. There was the music, sure, but he also needed a way to just use words. Pan was sorry Raliv felt this way, but Raliv had also sounded a hopeful note, one of having new experiences to lay over the top of his grief. Isn't that exactly what Pan had undertaken when he spent all that time in the mountains and then later, along the coast, and now, somewhere in the Midwest? Pan looked towards the farmhouse.

"Your friend," Raliv had signed it.

Pan pressed his lips together and strode back to camp to dry his boots. Along the way, he spied a set of shed antlers along the edge of the meadow about twenty yards away from each other. They were perfect. He hoped Raliv could use them. They were too bulky for Pan to carry around as he travelled, although he was tempted. If he found a buyer, they were worth some money. But he didn't know any buyers around these parts. They were all out west, in the mountains. No, Raliv could use them. He could hang them in his cabin, maybe, as decoration, or maybe a lamp. Pan had seen lamps made from antlers in stores.

Pan pulled off his soggy boots and put them by the fire and draped his worn-out socks on sticks above the flames. He pulled on the new dry socks and marveled at how wonderful something so simple could feel. He sat on a tree fall, wriggling his toes in his new socks, and carved on the little pieces of wood. That night he ate half a rabbit he snared earlier in the day and munched on celery and carrots. He felt like a rich man. The night was not nearly so cold as the previous few nights and he slept soundly with his socks on.

Pan was awakened by the sound of a rustling near his hut. He should have brought the antlers in with him. The squirrels would eat into them in no time. He climbed out and two squirrels darted off in opposite directions. He was just in time. There were no gnaw marks on the antlers.

Then Pan looked around him and saw that it was already shaping up to be a warm day. Sunlight was streaming through the branches that each day had more leaves opening up on them. A brown thrasher was singing from somewhere above him. His friend Karen had said a thrasher was a symbol of free will, that when someone hears a brown thrasher, they then know they can choose the path they want to take, even if it is difficult.

The forest came alive with bird songs now, as if they all knew they were greeting a spring day. A scarlet tanager echoed his song somewhere deep in the woods. An acadian flycatcher chirruped its chirps somewhere close.

Pan started up his fire again and heated up the remaining rabbit, watching the small flames flicker around the meat. The warmer temperatures stirred in him his desire to move on. Days like these were good days to move, warm but not too warm, dry, and with songbirds all around. Which path would he take, the one to the mountains, or the one the brown thrasher opened for him?

He tried to picture it while he ate the rabbit and followed it with an apple. It wasn't that much food, but he felt quite full. He wanted to head over to the chair and leave the antlers, but he wanted to write a note first. He wanted to tell Raliv that it wasn't unusual to discover new ways to hurt and that he would always have the love of Colleen, the same way Pan would always have the love of his son.

He sat on the log that had become his spot next to the little fire and wrote out the note, using his knee as a desk. When he wrote Colleen's name, he looked up from his writing, watching absently the tiny rivulets of water heading for a stream, then a creek, the river, and the ocean, eventually, only to be caught up in a tandem of wind and sun and carried back to join another rivulet somewhere.

It felt odd to him to use her name. Was it too intrusive? Perhaps names were more important sometimes.

He returned to his note. He also wanted to tell the old man how much he enjoyed his music. Then he looked up again, distracted by nothing more than a faint breeze. He was torn. He had made a friend here, and he had so very few anymore, but he also knew he needed to go, and he knew where he needed to go. He signed his note, "Your dear friend," then the name Raliv had given him, which he thought he would use for a long time.

Pan whittled carefully on the two pieces of wood, working on the finer points now, holding the large knife close to its tip to maneuver the small lines. He let the minutes slip by, the warmer weather lulling him and the goal of the carving distracting him.

When he did make his way up the deer path through the woods, he dropped off the antlers and the note, but instead of hiding in the trees and watching, he walked farther away, deeper into the stand of hardwoods to where a robin was sitting on a nest. He had heard the bird calling and was considering harvesting the eggs in the nest, a neat circle sitting on a maple branch within Pan's reach. She would probably have another brood later in the year, so it wouldn't be that bad to take the eggs.

Pan tiptoed to try to peer over the edge of the nest when the male robin suddenly swooped down and grazed his head, giving out a high-pitched squeak. Pan ducked and scooted farther away from the nest. The bird dived at him a second time and Pan retreated towards the field. He would leave the eggs alone. He stopped beneath a black walnut tree and brushed back his gray hair from where the bird had struck him.

Then he heard the recorder being played over by the chair. The song started out similar to the last little concert but quickly evolved into something different, something that he doubted he himself could play, and he had been playing his own flute for years.

Pan stood still, listening to the soft notes echo across the countryside. A soft breeze rustled the grasses. Across the field and into the woods, a woodpecker drummed a beat. The shadow of an osprey floated across the meadow, a dark dance to the hauntingly beautiful song. Then the tune wound to a close and he heard the truck grumble off onto the narrow road through the woods towards the cabin. Pan slipped over to the chair.

There was some rope there, strong jute rope. He draped it over his shoulder and read the note. Raliv was getting out, his note said. He was reaching out to family and friends and Pan was glad for that. But the old man still had questions that anyone has during such times, Pan guessed. It would be helpful if there were concrete answers to such difficult issues, but there simply aren't, and recognizing that might help Raliv.

Pan looked off into the sky to where the osprey had circled away. He wanted to say it just right. He would need to weigh his words carefully before writing them down. He returned his attention to the note. Raliv doesn't know what to play? Pan shook his head. Why in the world would he say that? His playing was beautiful and uniquely his.

Perhaps that was the problem, that Raliv as so many others think that they have to sound like everyone else rather than to write their own melodies, woven from the tapestry of their worlds. Pan shook his head in disbelief. And there, the last part, where Raliv picked up on Pan's itchy feet. But he said Pan was welcome to come back.

Now he nodded his head. He believed just that moment he would absolutely be back to visit with Raliv, to listen to the old man play his flute, and to check on his well-being. Yes, he would be back. How different it would be then.

Pan walked across the old pasture towards his camp. Raliv had driven his truck, so he would hear if he returned. He dropped off the rope in his hut and picked up his little fishing pole that he had rolled beneath his sitting log. If eggs were off the menu, perhaps it was time to try his hand at fishing in the beaver pond. He took his little stringer and made his was around the side of the hill towards the pond.

Leaves were budding out on every branch. A squirrel leaped from one treetop to another in the canopy above him. As he approached the pond, a frog jumped from the bank into the water with a splash. He swung the sardine-lid lure back and forth over the nesting fish that attacked the shiny spoon just like the robin had attacked Pan. He had four nice-sized bluegill on his stringer when he heard a twig snap on the other side of the pond. A great blue heron squawked off and Pan stepped back into the cottonwood trees with his pole and his stringer in hand.

He had nearly been caught unaware. The old man was very comfortable in these woods. And maybe Pan was getting less cautious. That in itself was reason enough to move on. He watched Raliv sit on a log and toss a stone, lost in thought. Pan watched him for just a moment, then backed out of the trees and into the brush beyond. He did not need to intrude on Raliv's space, even if the old man would have no clue he was there. Pan had wanted privacy when he was reflective; he figured Raliv might as well.

Pan cooked the fish over an open fire and boiled some tender lamb's quarters he had found along the creek bank. He added another celery stalk to his meal and believed he could almost feel himself strengthening, ready to make his journey.

When it grew dark, he pulled the warmed stone into his hut to warm his bedding and went out to sit by the small campfire he was letting burn down. It was a very pleasant evening, so he sat by the fire next to the little stream, listening to a barred owl off in the distance. Far off, atop a ridge a mile or more away, he heard the train whistle blow, the same train he heard every night.

Raliv also had a fire going in his fireplace, Pan could smell. Pan once had a home with a fireplace, a home he could recall clearly. But just now, he saw Raliv's cabin, the oil lamp on the desk, the little kitchen with the woodstove, the maple table. But there were no coasters to protect the furniture.

Pan smiled. He went to the lean-to he slept in and retrieved the rope Raliv had given him. He sat by his own fire and tied several lengths of the rope into the intricate knot his son had taught him to tie when he had been home on leave. He worked slowly, deliberately, tracing the tagline through the loops. He pictured them in Raliv's little cabin, on the little table by his chair maybe.

One day, perhaps Pan would sit in the other chair and they would talk. Or play music together. Or maybe look into the flames of the fireplace, each of them lost in thought, but found in each other's company. Possibly, occasionally, they would speak.

What would Pan say to his friend? He tried to imagine. Raliv had a son. He had mentioned it in a note. Maybe they could talk about sons before the fire.

Pan's throat tightened.

But right now, Raliv was saying he wanted answers, although Pan saw he was looking for solutions, not answers. There is a difference, Pan knew. That's what he needed to tell his friend. Riddles have answers, even if we sometimes don't know them until we live them. And he needed to stop feeling guilty. Was that his advice to Raliv or himself? His eyes watered a bit, but maybe it was smoke from the little campfire. He finished tying the second knot, then crawled into his hut and slept as the fire burned out.

Pan was out early. He had work to do on his one last project.

Pan and the Message Chair

He had left the two coasters and his note on the chair and walked back to the walnut tree when he heard the song on the recorder. From where he stood along the edge of the meadow, he could just see Raliv, swaying back and forth on the chair, playing, his eyes closed in focus. Pan was far enough away that he saw Raliv lower his flute just a moment before the melody stopped.

Then Raliv walked away and climbed into the truck, which growled to life. Pan heard the faint sound of a cat meowing as the old man drove away.

Pan walked along the edge of the woods, then across to the chair. On the chair was a small tarp, tightly folded. It would be so much better than a trash bag. A tarp was as good as a tent, really, and more versatile. It was an absolute extravagance.

Pan picked up the note and read. The old man was making recorders for grandkids now. That made Pan smile. Then he read the part where Raliv felt lucky to have won his wife's love. And, he had written he forgave himself. Pan looked out across the little pond. Forgiving oneself was so very difficult. Now Pan looked towards the farmhouse. He sat there for a long time, watching the grasses bow and bob.

The meadow was turning green from the bottom up and he could see the new grasses beginning to push forth. He would miss the letters too, but it was time He heard power tools somewhere near the farmhouse and it shook him from his reverie. He walked behind the pine tree he had taken shelter from and picked up some cones and fallen pine needle and headed back to camp. He needed a gift that could remind the old man of Pan's having been there. He would part with some of his herbs.

Pan worked feverishly on his projects back at his rough camp. He thought about what to say to Raliv in his note. Karen had told him that whenever he said her name, she would know it, even though they might be far apart. She had told him that so he could remember her, so she could remain in his thoughts, and, thus, remain.

Pan cut a patch from a tired work shirt with his knife and washed it in the stream. He perched the small cloth on a couple of sticks and gathered together the herbs he had learned to gather to keep his ruck sack smelling clean. He had learned it from her.

"Karen," he said aloud. His voice cracked, the speaking being so different. "Karen," he said again, his voice clearer. He looked at the stand of sycamore trees. "Bobby." Pan swallowed hard.

Pan ate the last of the vegetables he had received and wrote his note to Raliv. He knew what he wanted to say, how anything that is hollowed out can be filled, eventually. And he would let Raliv know he was leaving the day after tomorrow. He would tell him when, and he would see his friend one last time before he left.

He would leave the note and the herbs tomorrow then start breaking down his camp. He had a few finishing touches to make on one last project. But then he would scatter the hut, erase the fire pit with water and sand. He would use the tarp for shelter for one night, maybe enjoy that other can of sardines, then he would go, and no one would be able to tell he had been there.

The nights were warmer now, so he didn't need a fire. But of course, Raliv would know he had been there. He had lots of evidence, the evidence that Pan hoped the old man would hold onto and share with others when the time came. Pan crawled into his hut one last time and slept.

The next day was busy. He scattered everything into the woods, the leaves, the stray branches used to insulate his hovel, the pine needles he had used to soften the bedding area. It had been a good shelter, primarily because he had managed to stay dry in it, for the most part. He left his letter and the sachet on the chair and only returned to the chair to get Raliv's drawing later. The old man could draw, too. Pan shook his head in appreciative wonder.

Back at his camp, Pan repacked his rucksack, so much more tightly filled than before. When he did, he reread the letter, this time from beginning to end. He nodded his head and pressed his lips together. He finished working on his last gift, sitting by the little waterway in the woods. He admired his handiwork and set it aside.

He was ready to go.

He still had some salted squirrel from before, and dandelions were up all over. He had what he needed. He slept under the tarp, using it as a thin crinkly blanket atop his other thin quilts. The next morning, he sat on his favorite log, watching the water trickle along. He listened to the forest come alive around him. A squirrel barked at him from a hickory tree. He turned his face to the sky and felt the sunlight warm him.

As the sun climbed, he gathered his sack and his own walking stick and walked to the chair. He left his final note to his friend Raliv and his one last gift. He hoped the note could express what he felt, and that it would somehow resonate with Raliv. In it, he said goodbye. Then he stood along the tree line and waited and listened.

Chapter 16
Raliv

Raliv woke up early, a pale pink light on his face. He opened his eyes and there was the crystal in the geode, gleaming in the morning sunlight, refracting the light into his face. Well, there are worse ways to wake up, he supposed, like having a cat jump on him and then kneading his chin and purring until he opened his eyes.

But the truth was, he didn't really mind Felicity's form of alarm clock either. It only meant she missed him. He sat up. He hoped Felicity was fine, and he knew she would be. She was very self-sufficient. He sat on the edge of the bed and smelled the faint odor of lavender. He nodded and stood. That wasn't unpleasant at all. He could not recall any dream and thought about the dreamcatcher hanging on his bed post at the house.

"Huh," he sighed aloud. He checked the cellphone he had put beside the bed the night before. Seven-thirty. There was lots of time before midday. He built a fire in the cookstove then started the coffee. Once he had that going, he went out to the outhouse beyond the tool shed and came back and washed his hands at the sink.

He had not thought to bring anything for breakfast, so he stepped into the pantry and scanned the shelves. He was tempted by the sardines and kippered herring, but not the Vienna sausages. Next to the Vienna sausages, along the right-hand side about chin high, he saw where Colleen had stored the packets of single serving canned ham. Colleen had bought them in case there was a natural disaster, her reasoning being the stuff would survive intact almost any sort of disaster short of nuclear war, and perhaps even that.

He took a packet out into the kitchen area, opened it, and slid the slice out into a skillet he had put on the stove top. The coffee was gurgling next to the skillet. The boys had scoffed at the canned ham but Raliv knew, when you have the appetite, it can fit the bill.

He could see the coffee perking up through the glass top of the percolator. It was plenty dark. Using a tea towel as a hot pad, he lifted the pot off the stove top and onto a trivet on the countertop to let the grounds settle a moment before pouring it. He flipped the ham slice and waited for the other side to sear a little before scooping it onto a plate. He squirted a dollop of coarse brown mustard onto the plate and then poured a cup of deep brown-black coffee and took all of it to the picnic table.

It was chilly outside, but not so cool he could not enjoy being there with the earthy, bitter coffee and the salty, rich ham. Colleen's flowers had bounced back from the snow and various colors of daylilies were sending out their heads, ready to bloom any day.

One more gift, Pan had said. Raliv considered just what that might be Pan mentioned so specifically. And maybe Raliv was going to actually meet Pan, or at least see them. That in itself would be a gift.

All the presents had been wonderful. Raliv recounted the list as he sat there eating his ham slowly. Pan had split a cord of wood that would last Raliv for months, especially now that warmer weather was here. There was the dreamcatcher that seemed to work, although Raliv being open both to the idea of its working and to encouraging himself to have the dreams no doubt helped. And Raliv loved the light that came through the geode and the smell of the sachet.

Pan and the Message Chair

These gifts were the kinds of things Colleen would have enjoyed in the cabin as well, but he realized they also were things that Raliv alone had added to the cabin and the farmhouse. Yes, they were presents from Pan, but Raliv had added them to the space. These were ways that the cabin and the farm were different now, and although Raliv knew Colleen would approve, these additions were his doing.

It felt odd, as if he were rearranging their world, if ever so slightly. He wasn't erasing anything, but he was adding to the world they had built in a way that he knew Colleen would like. Ultimately, it was his doing alone. It was what he had to do with his life, he knew. He could add to the world they had built without ever taking anything away. He returned to his mental listing.

There was the wonderful peppery arugula he had enjoyed and that had encouraged him to fix the special meal that night. In fact, he had started doing a lot more cooking now. The presents had all started with the rabbit bag which hung now by the backdoor of the farmhouse, a simple gift that took hours and hours to make, between catching and skinning the rabbits to tanning the hides to stitching it all together.

Then, when Raliv had pulled the muscle in his back, it was Pan's liniment that had helped him loosen it up. Raliv thought of the walking stick that was the perfect size for Raliv. That was here at the cabin too, just inside the pantry, on the right side next to the fishing pole. He gave himself a smile. Colleen would be proud. And the beautiful coasters he had used for his wine glass the night before were still on the little table between the chairs. The antlers that were going to make his mud-foyer bench something extra special for Raliv were already there, leaning up against the pieces of wood.

He decided he wanted to take all of it to the house and show John tonight and then the rest of his family tomorrow afternoon. It would be his way of telling them the story so they too could maybe understand what a wonderful friend Pan was, how quickly Pan had understood who Raliv was and what would be an appropriate or even needed gift.

He had wondered before how to tell his family about this mysterious friend – the gifts would be a perfect way to broach the story. Raliv wanted to remember what he had given to Pan too, in part because he knew his family would be curious, but also because it would speak to how mutual the friendship had become.

Now he mentally listed his own gifts to Pan. He had let Pan stay inside the cabin, for one. There were sardines and fishing tackle. String, fruits and vegetables, socks, a tarp. What else? Oh yes, the paper and pen that had made the messages able to continue. The jute rope was another gift and finally the drawing he had done that he gave Pan yesterday.

No, that would not be the final gift. The song that Raliv had practiced last night would be the final gift, at least until Pan returned, which he knew would happen. Raliv wanted very much to make the song speak to Pan about Raliv's friendship, about Raliv himself, for that matter, so that Pan would be able to remember him all the better.

Thinking about that reminded Raliv of the most amazing gift he had received of all of them - the recorder. Raliv found so much pleasure in playing the little flute. He loved the sound it made and how already he had found ways to change the sound by breathing both in and out and running his tongue across the mouthpiece as he played in a kind of la-la-la. Sometimes he even made "S" sounds and "CH" sounds while playing, experimenting with the different effects. Other times, he just ran his fingers over the holes, feathering the sound until it came across as birds singing in the brush. He covered up the edge of the hole and made sounds like the wind in the leaves of the trees as they breathed in the summer.

In fact, Raliv had to admit the flute was a present he appreciated as much as any gift he had ever received. It was as if Raliv was finding a way to put his now changed world into some sort of perspective by playing the recorder. He could say things with his music he did not have words for, and that empowered him and strengthened him in a manner he could not have anticipated. He decided he wanted to practice some more before the midday playing. And he needed to gather the gifts.

He stood and took his cup and plate back inside. He cleaned the plate and dried it and put it away. He poured a second cup of strong coffee and set it on one of the Turk's knot coasters by his chair where he would practice, but first, he went to the desk and retrieved all the notes from Pan, even the very first few that had been hard to read because the paper was tiny.

He had kept them all in the drop front desk. He pulled them out and sorted through them. Putting them in order of when he had received them, he then secured them together with a large paper clip. If he was going to show off the gifts, what better gifts had Pan given Raliv than the advice, the warmth, the caring of supportive words?

Raliv played on the recorder and finished his coffee. He had no idea how long he had been playing. When he checked the cell phone, it was ten o'clock. It wasn't midday, but it had gotten closer and Raliv felt a slight urgency to get organized. He shoved the phone into his pocket. He hurried around the house, cleaning up the coffee pot, filling the bird feeder, and closing up the firebox to extinguish any last embers in the stove. He loaded Pan's handwritten messages and the gifts that he still had in the cabin into the SUV. He wanted them to be part of this space ultimately, but he could bring them back out. He put the little packet of notes on the passenger seat.

He would not be able to write a note to Pan today. Pan had said so, that they were leaving after giving Raliv one more present. Raliv would have to say his goodbye in the song that he played. That was all the chance he would have, at least for now. As he loaded the car, a wren gibed from hawthorn bush, then darted away into the woods. Raliv decided he would go to the house first and take all the gifts in. He could take care of Felicity and then return to the chair in time to play for Pan.

Raliv realized "midday" was not necessarily noon if someone doesn't own a clock and he seriously doubted Pan carried a watch of any sort. No, midday would mean when the sun was high and nothing more, and Raliv was not going to miss this opportunity.

He closed the cabin door and started to lock it but decided not to. In fact, he might not ever lock it again. What if Pan came through sometime in the future and it was late, and they needed a place to sleep? And no one bothered the place. No one really even knew it was there. Colleen and Raliv had not broadcast it around and other than the fellow who built it, and he had no reason to talk about it, no one had a clue it was there; it was just a cabin deep in the woods above a beaver pond. But Pan knew about it, and that meant a lot.

Raliv climbed into the car and drove up the path, across the low spots along the ridge that kept at least a little mud in them until the dog days of summer, and into the meadow. It was early yet. There was nothing on the chair. Good.

The grass was greening beneath the waves of switchgrass. An osprey soared above, using only subtle movements of its wings to change course. The daffodils were full bloomed now. He drove on past, turned through the opening and pulled up to the farmhouse. He carried all the gifts in carefully, making several trips. He did not want to drop anything. He arranged them all on the kitchen table.

Felicity jumped into the window and watched him move as if bemused by so much activity. Raliv arranged the presents by size, then decided by order of his receiving them made more sense in telling the story. He retrieved the dreamcatcher and the pinch pot of ointment from the bedroom, and picked up the antlers from where he had leaned them against the mock-up of the mud-foyer bench. Where was the rabbit bag? Oh yes, hanging on the peg by the door. He had eaten the arugula, of course, and he would just have to tell the part about the firewood being split, but it was an impressive array of wonderful, handmade gifts.

Pan and the Message Chair

Raliv stood for a moment, surveying the collection. He wished Colleen could see it. She too would have marveled at the artistry of the handiwork and the thoughtfulness of each gift.

He put the small stack of messages on the edge of the table. He was ready to tell the story. He really wished he could tell Colleen all about Pan, and maybe he already had, in his own way. Maybe he could tell her about Pan when he played the song at the message chair. It would be a song for Pan and a song for Colleen. What better song could Raliv play? He was excited about his tiny concert coming up. He would have the best audience he could imagine.

Felicity hopped down onto the floor with a thump. Raliv's moment of reflection was evidently no longer keeping her amused. Raliv's reverie was broken by the movement of the cat. She rolled over for a petting. Raliv walked across the kitchen, leaned over, and pet her. Taking it as a kind of reminder, Raliv checked the water and food for the calico, washed up, then looked at the clock in the kitchen. Not yet eleven. How could time pass so slowly?

He decided he had time to assemble the recorders he had made for the grandchildren. That was a good short-term project. It wouldn't take long. He could do that and then head to the chair. He took his own recorder and the keys and went to outside. The forsythia had burst forth in the last couple of days, a profusion of lemony yellow blossoms and bright light green leaves on long tendrils of ochre. A house finch balanced on one swaying arch of the bush, his deep red head contrasting with the cadmium yellow blossoms.

Raliv put his recorder in the truck then went to the workshop. The mouthpieces were carved and ready. He had only to twist them together and test them out. He also wanted to decorate them a bit with some turns of jute twine and some fancy knots of some sort.

The recorders worked great. He was looking forward to teaching the grandchildren "Au Clair de la Lune," which had been easy enough for him to learn. And he had the little music box with the tune to reinforce it all. He carried the little instruments to the back porch and left them on a wicker table by the lawn chair, then went out and climbed into the truck and started towards the chair.

He realized that his heart was pounding.

He parked in the dirt path and opened the door. There was something on the chair, alright. He made his way over to it. It was one of the sardine cans from that very first day, but the top had been folded in and flattened, and now, it was a bed. Inside the tin bed were two carved wooden figures, eyes closed, sleeping under a pale blue patch of cloth.

It was Raliv and Colleen, of course. The one figure had white hair and a white beard, painted onto the textured wood by what looked to be crushed up limestone. The other figure had deep brown hair that curled around her face. Raliv inspected the piece closely. The hair was painted with the color from walnut hulls, from the smell of it. The carving was so intricate, so delicate, that there was no mistaking exactly who the two figurines represented. Pan had used the photo, of course, and knew the color of the blanket from experience.

The little piece looked exactly to Raliv like he and Colleen sleeping in the cabin bed. Pan had even gotten the correct side of the bed, but then, Raliv supposed, they had a fifty-fifty chance of that. How many times over the years had he stood next to that cabin bed, watching her sleep? She would sometimes awaken and tell him to stop, worrying that somehow her unkempt sleepy hair or some awkward position she may have held her mouth while asleep was off-putting or unattractive, but nothing could have been farther from the truth. Even asleep, Colleen was beautiful.

And Pan had done a very good job capturing her likeness. How many hours of careful whittling would it have taken to make this? Raliv wanted to put it on the mantle next to the photo at the cabin so that once again, whenever he wanted to, he could watch her sleep next to him. But first he wanted to show it to John and Brian and all of his family. It was such a heartfelt gift, a reminder of his peaceful sleep with Colleen, a time when all of the illness had been far away.

The two little figures slept peacefully in their tiny sardine can bed. Raliv's throat knotted. It was perfect.

Raliv picked up the note that had been under the carving. He realized his hand was shaking just a bit.

He sat on the chair and read.

My dear friend Raliv,

Thank you for your beautiful drawing of the eastern wood pewee. It is wonderfully done. You have so many talents. I love how you captured the movement, the life of the bird. Being an artist is believing in life, I think, and your piece shows that. There is something in the moment you have captured that could not be expressed any other way. I will treasure it.

You mentioned in your last note about what life means, and embedded in that question is what death means. This is what I think it all means. I saw you walking the other day and you stopped to toss a pebble into the pond. When threw the rock, it made a ripple. The fish beneath the water likely started, then floated back to where they had been. The ripple spread across the water, licking at a log, perhaps moistening the feet of a turtle on the log. A frog sitting on the water lily maybe felt her platform waver. Eventually it affected everything it passed. Everything was changed just a little bit because that ripple went through. Then it reached the shore and you could see the ripple. You could have measured it if you wanted to. You could even have found its force and its starting and stopping places using math. But once it hit the shore, the ripple was gone. The ripple was gone, but the water is still there. The water has just returned to being the pond the way it always was and that's what life is. Each one of our lives is like a ripple and our souls are part of the water. Our souls for a time are in this life or in that life or in that ripple or splash, but in the end, we return to being the water.

That's the way I see it anyway.

I wanted you to have this little sculpture as a reminder of the life you shared with Colleen. I know she means the world to you. I hope having this little image will help you enjoy your many memories. Embrace them. You will have times of loneliness. That is certain. Perhaps in those times, this piece will help you through.

Pan and the Message Chair

I am looking forward to hearing your song. Always play to the valley and maybe I will pick up a part of the song with you.

Until we meet again, I remain,

Your friend,

Pan

Raliv read through the note twice, remembering his walk down to the pond. He might have felt spied upon, but instead he felt protected, sheltered by the watchful eye of Pan. His throat was even tighter now, and his eyes were moist. He sighed deeply, trying to get his breath, and trying to calm his emotions some.

He twisted in the chair until he was facing the long row of trees that marked the descent into the valley. Lifting the recorder to his mouth, he began to play. An instant later, he heard his notes echo from the valley.

He smiled as he played. "Always play to the valley and maybe I will pick up a part of the song with you." Raliv played his farewell song. It was a song full of twirls and twists, a song that expressed just how happy Raliv was to have met Pan. All of it echoed back to him as if he were playing in a concert hall.

The melody now became a song about Colleen, and he played long, low notes that he poured as much love into as possible. He included fragments of her favorite tunes and a floating sequence that he thought might capture the twinkle in her eyes. Ah, those eyes. He played the brightness in her eyes and her laughter and the sound of her beautiful singing. And then he added notes about the world he had built with Colleen, a world he welcomed his new friend into. It had the sound of bird whistles and tree frogs and the low, reassuring sound of the earth turning beneath his feet and the trees leafing out, each tree a different rhythm. He played psithurisms and raindrops and all of the sounds of the beautiful life he had shared with Colleen.

Tears streamed down Raliv's face. Through it all, he watched the tree line. He blinked away the tears. There. Halfway down the hill just at the edge of the forest. He thought he saw something move. Was it Pan? Did he just see someone step out from the tree line, or is it only one of the trees themselves, swaying slightly in the wind?

No, while it is clad in the color of tree trunks, this slender trunk has a face that is now looking at Raliv, giving him a smile and a nod, and then stepping back into the woods as quietly and stealthily as a zephyr.

Raliv quickly ran the image back into his mind as he kept playing. Pan was tall. Very tall. A very tall man, from the looks of him. His face and hair had been surrounded by leaves and his clothes were various faded shades of grey. His ability to not be seen was clear – he looked like a tree. He looked like a tree with warm, tender brown eyes. The eyes were the color of an acorn.

Raliv had seen him.

He was nearing the end of his song and he wanted to say one last goodbye, but he didn't know how far Pan had moved away already so he gave one last blast on his recorder, one that would have sent his old music teaching climbing the walls.

Then he heard a shrill note come from the woods.

That was no echo.

Chapter 17
Pan

Pan heard the rumble of the truck before he saw it, of course. Pan barely turned his head, watching the truck bounce to a stop. Raliv climbed out and picked up the piece Pan had carved and inspected it. The old man smiled and that made Pan smile.

Pan watched him read the note that he wished could say more, but it was done now. Then Raliv began playing. Pan closed his eyes and listened intently. It was a beautiful melody, but more than a melody. It was a pouring out of the man's joy and sorrow, a sound as pure as Pan had ever heard. Pan opened his eyes and watched as Raliv swayed back and forth on the chair, playing, crying, but every note belonged exactly where it was.

Then Pan stepped out into the meadow, just a bit, looked up the hillside to where Raliv sat. He saw Raliv's eyes open wide and that brought another smile to Pan's face. Then he stepped back into the woods and walked down the hill, to follow the trail across the countryside, up into the mountains and down again, and eventually along the stream to where it became the river, his river, Bobby's river.

The music grew fainter through the leafing forest. Then he heard the shriek of a note, Raliv's goodbye. He put his recorder to his mouth and blew hard, to say, "Until next time, my friend."

Epilogue

The four children scrambled on ahead of Raliv, the youngest one trailing behind the older three. They all gripped their recorders and scurried around the catalpa tree towards the chair. The sun smiled down on the five of them. A small breeze tousled the children's hair as they half-ran, half-stumbled, in the case of the younger ones trying to keep up, across the field of tall swaying grasses.

Raliv walked behind, swinging his walking stick in rhythm to his steps. He carried his little flute in his other hand. All four of the grandchildren were at the chair now, trying to sit at the same time on it. The chair was almost wide enough for all four, but not quite, so that their struggle to fit on it was a constant game of musical chair. The youngest was the most secure on the chair – none of the other three would push her off - but the others struggled with each other for space. It was good natured for now, but Raliv knew eventually someone would get their feelings hurt.

He made his way to the chair, put his recorder in his pocket and leaned the walking stick against the back of the chair. He reached down and picked up Megan, the youngest. The other three filled the spot immediately and with great satisfaction.

"No." Raliv leaned forward. "I need you all to stand on the chair. Okay?" JJ led the way by standing up on the seat. Joey and Becky followed suit. If there was not room for all four to sit, there was room for them to stand. Raliv put Megan down to stand on the seat with the others.

"Grandad, tell us again about Pan." Becky looked up, her eyes bright with curiosity. The entire family had been deeply engrossed in the story, but it seemed to Raliv that Becky was the one who was truly captivated by Raliv's friendship with Pan.

"I will, but a little later." He steadied Megan. "Right now, we have a concert to play."

He had taught the children the first few notes of "Au Clair de la Lune." They didn't know all of it, and what they did know was, of course, uneven. Joey seemed to take to the little flute the fastest and was playing it on his own while the Legos and cars and action figures occupied the others. "Okay, everyone get your flutes ready. Remember, face the valley, and maybe Pan will hear us and play along with us."

JJ turned and the others followed his lead. Raliv took his own recorder out and lifted it up. "Ready? We're going to play what we learned twice through." The children lifted up their instruments. "One. Two. Three. Play."

What came out was a mishmash of notes, of course. Raliv wanted to laugh at the discordance. With three of the five being somewhat on track, it was possible to make out the melody, but just barely. The four grandchildren followed Raliv's playing, so they were always just a little behind, except for Megan, who was not playing anything that sounded familiar, but Raliv didn't care.

As they first started, the notes echoed back and Raliv saw a smile creep across JJ's face, getting the joke the same way Raliv had. When they finished the little sequence of notes, Becky gave a blast on her recorder, just as Raliv had recounted in the story, and the other four, Raliv included, blew as hard as they could also.

The whistle floated off through the trees and carried on the wind down to the creek at the bottom of the hill. On a large red oak tree, a barred owl opened his eyes, turned his head, and blinked.

About the Author

Lawrence has six books in print, four novels, one memoir, and one nonfiction. He has a contract for three more. He writes literary novels, short fiction, non-fiction articles and books, creative non-fiction, and poetry.

His work has appeared in a wide range of local, regional, and national journals. He also is a visual artist working in graphite, oils, metal and wood. Dr. Weill lives in the woods in Kentucky overlooking a beaver pond next to a wildlife preserve. He is also an avid outdoorsman and gardener.

Made in United States
North Haven, CT
01 June 2023